THE ESCARPMENT

Also by Ron Base

Fiction

Matinee Idol
Foreign Object
Splendido
Magic Man
The Strange
The Sanibel Sunset Detective
The Sanibel Sunset Detective Returns
Another Sanibel Sunset Detective
The Two Sanibel Sunset Detectives
The Hound of the Sanibel Sunset Detective
The Confidence Man
The Sanibel Sunset Detective Goes to London

Non-fiction

The Movies of the Eighties (with David Haslam)
If the Other Guy Isn't Jack Nicholson, I've Got the Part
Marquee Guide to Movies on Video
Cuba Portrait of an Island (with Donald Nausbaum)

www.ronbase.com
Read Ron's blog at
www.ronbase.wordpress.com
Contact Ron at
ronbase@ronbase.com

THE ESCARPMENT

A Novel of Suspense

Ron Base

Copyright © 2016 Ron Base

Library and Archives Canada Cataloguing in Publication

Base, Ron, 1948-, author

The escarpment / Ron Base.

ISBN 978-0-9940645-2-3 (paperback)

I. Title.

PS8553.A784E84 2016   C813'.54   C2016-903946-3

Publisher's Note: This is a work of fiction. Names, characters, places, and incidents either are products of the author's imagination or are used fictitiously. Any
resemblance to actual persons, events, or locales is entirely coincidental.

West-End Books
133 Mill St.
Milton, Ontario
L9T 1S1

Cover design and co-ordination: Jennifer Smith
Text design and electronic formatting: Ric Base
Author photograph: Katherine Lenhoff

First Edition

For Rebecca and Kim

Readers should know there is a real place called Milton. From Toronto, you drive west an hour or so (depending on traffic), turn south on Highway 25, and soon you have reached the town. That's the real Milton. The Milton you read about in the following pages, while accurate insofar as setting, is, nonetheless, a fictional Milton, the Milton out of this author's slightly diabolical imagination. That's what writers do, of course; they make things up. What follows is the made-up Milton; the characters here do not exist, the incidents described never happened.

PROLOGUE

An hour before her life fell apart, RCMP Corporal Jean Whitlock and Sergeant Adam Machota celebrated the success of the raid.

The restaurant was not far from Camp Nathan Smith where they had been headquartered for the past seven months. The restaurant was known for the roast chicken that Sergeant Machota liked, and the lamb meatballs that she favored. They both enjoyed the *bulani*, Afghan fried bread pockets stuffed with vegetables.

Sergeant Machota tore off a piece of the *bulani* and dipped it into a bowl of yogurt as he said, "Good day's work, Corporal Whitlock. Damn good day's work."

"I actually feel like there's a reason for us being here," Jean Whitlock said.

Machota grinned. "Hey, don't get too carried away."

Nonetheless, the raid on a warehouse located at the outskirts of Kandahar City had gone much better than anyone expected. The Afghan National Police (ANP) had actually done the job they were supposed to do, the job the Mounties were there to train them for. It was Jean's guy, Major Shaar Zorn, who had received the tip that ten tons of hashish were coming across the border from neighboring Tajikistan. The hashish was hidden in shipments of particle board. Five Afghan men had been arrested without a shot being fired. Textbook stuff.

Now they were relaxing, a celebration of sorts before they left Kandahar. During the meal, Jean, despite herself, couldn't help but train her eyes on Sergeant Machota. In his mid-thirties, he was the poster boy for the kind of rock-jawed Mountie hero she had imagined when she was growing up.

Sergeant Machota's dark, perfectly aligned looks caused everyone to call him Dudley Do Right although no one doubted his abilities. Machota was easy on the eyes but everyone knew he was also fast-tracked for greater things. Afghanistan was rumored to be the next stepping stone for him. Today's raid certainly wouldn't hurt his future prospects.

"You've done well out here," Machota said to her. "A lot of guys—and these are guys, mind you—got here and couldn't handle it. Two men I know no sooner landed than the bullets started to fly, and they freaked out, begged to be sent home. Goddamn embarrassing. I hear the day you got here, a helicopter blew up right in front of you. Instead of running for cover, you were organizing your people to help the wounded and prepare for another attack. Impressive."

"That's not to say I wasn't scared and didn't think about jumping on the first plane home," Jean said. "What you're not prepared for, I think, is the lack of control. You come from an environment in which you are basically in control of a situation. Here, not only are you not in control, but there are lots of people out to kill you."

"Yeah, it's a bitch," Machota said. "But tell me about yourself, Corporal Whitlock. How did you get so tough and well-organized? Where are you from?"

"A small town in Ontario called Milton," Jean answered, digging into the meatballs. "Not exactly a place where I had to be tough, although my brother might disagree. He claims I used to beat him up as a kid."

"Milton?" Machota said. "Never heard of it."

"It's about forty-five minutes west of Toronto, just below the Niagara Escarpment."

Machota dipped another piece of bread into the yogurt as he said, "I'm from a small town, too, northern British Columbia where my old man had a small logging business. Tough old bugger. He had me and my brother out working in thirty degree below weather when we were fourteen. We didn't pay a whole lot of attention to what went on back East."

"Sounds pretty rough," Jean said.

"At the time it was all I knew. You worked. You ate. You slept. Who knew there was anything else?"

"But you got out?"

"A tree fell on my old man, and that was that. I had to look around for something else. Figured being a Mountie was easier than dragging logs down the side of a mountain."

"Milton was still a sleepy little farming town when I grew up there," Jean said. "But that's all changed. It's become a suburb of Toronto, and even though it still feels like a small town to me, it is in fact the fastest-growing community in Canada—at least it is according to my brother."

"Everything's changing," Machota said with a shake of his head. "Everything's getting bigger and more complicated. Hard for a logger's kid to keep up. You looking forward to going home?"

"I suppose so," Jean said. "Except I'm not sure where home is. If you mean, do I want to go back to Milton, no."

"No?"

"That's why I joined the Force. So I could get out of there."

"So you could be here in Kandahar, trying to convince ANP guys that killing your wife or marrying your ten-year-old daughter off to a rich guy may not be such a good idea."

"I'd like to think we've made some progress out here," Jean said.

"Listen, speaking of progress," Machota said. "I forgot to mention it earlier, but Major Zorn has invited us back to his place for a farewell drink. He says he's got a good bottle of Oban Scotch waiting us."

"That's odd," Jean said. "He didn't say anything to me."

"I just got a text from him a couple of hours ago," Machota said.

"I'm not much of a Scotch drinker," Jean said.

"I'm sure he'd be glad to pour you some tea," Machota said. "Me, I'd like to get my hands on that Scotch. It's been a while. What do you say? I think it would be discourteous to refuse his invitation, don't you?"

"I like Major Zorn," Jean said. "I actually get the feeling he's listening when a woman speaks."

"He's listening when you speak. I'm not so sure about anyone else."

"He's a highly unusual man for this part of the world. It's very kind of him to invite us."

"It was a good day," Machota said.

"That it was," Jean said. "Seeing the Major and having a chance to say goodbye will put a nice finish to it."

Machota just smiled.

They drove in one of the armored G-wagons Machota seemed able to commandeer at will. The narrow Kandahar streets were dark and noisy nearing midnight. Machota dodged young men on mopeds, jerry-rigged pickup trucks, battered Toyotas that didn't look like they could start let alone travel on the road.

Machota drove with a confidence that bespoke a man who knew where he was going in this foreign place. When you were Adam Machota, Jean mused, the world somehow bent to your will—even in the very uncertain world of Kandahar City.

"Town this size," Machota mused aloud, "and not a single traffic light. Amazing."

Among the many, many amazing things here, Jean thought. Even in sun-blasted daylight, Kandahar remained the mystery that could never be solved—certainly not by a couple of visiting Canadians. What a joke to ever think they could.

They passed a security checkpoint and entered an upscale neighborhood, surprisingly quiet and lovely in contrast to the rest of the city. An orchard was just visible in the moonlight beyond a low wall. Traffic islands were choked with flowers and trees. They came onto a street of neat houses with red-tiled roofs. At the end, they turned into a drive flanked by lush lawns doused by sprinklers sending up sprays of water courtesy of the nearby Arghandab River.

"This is where the major lives?" Jean asked.

"This is it," Machota said.

"He lives very well."

"The major knows how to survive in this country," Machota said with a knowing grin. "Come on, let's get inside."

Jean grabbed her shoulder bag and slid out of the vehicle. As she followed Machota to the front entrance, she noticed the interior was in darkness. He opened the door and then stood aside for her to enter. She hesitated.

"Are you sure we can just walk in?"

"It's fine," he said. "He said we should make ourselves at home."

She went in and found herself in an unlit hallway. She heard the door close behind her. Abruptly, she was spun around and pushed back against the wall. She could barely make out Machota coming at her.

"What are you doing?" she managed to say, just before he mashed his mouth against hers, at the same time grabbing her by the throat.

"You like this," she heard him say.

His huge hand tightened its grip on her throat. She couldn't breathe. She tried to shake him off, but he was too strong. A moment later, his mouth pulled away. He slapped her hard across the face. She saw stars and gasped.

He ripped the front of her blouse open and tore at her bra. She screamed for him to stop. "You like this," he repeated, louder this time, as though trying to convince himself.

He struck her again. The force of the blow sent her sprawling onto the tile floor, surprisingly cool in the dimness. Her shoulder bag went flying, spewing its contents. He loomed over her, undoing his belt, pulling down his fly and exposing himself. She tried to roll away, but he caught her, clawing at her slacks, trying to pull them down her hips. She reached frantically across the floor, desperate to hold onto something, anything.

Machota slapped her again. Her head struck the tile and she saw more stars. Her fingers encountered something solid. She realized dimly that it was the expandable police baton she kept in her bag. Her hand closed around the hard rubber grip.

Machota, breathing hard, got off her and rose, pushing his pants and underpants down around his ankles.

Still down on the ground, she flicked the button on the baton so that it extended to its full twenty-six-inch length. She raised her am and whacked the extended baton against his groin.

He screamed and staggered away, bent over, holding himself.

Jean scrambled to her feet and slammed the baton against the side of his head. That sent him sprawling back on the floor. She pulled her Glock pistol from its holster on her belt just as the front door burst open. She glimpsed an armed man, raised the Glock, and fired. The man went down. Another gunman appeared, and Jean shot him too.

Behind her, she heard a back door smashing open. The sound of boots coming forward. Machota lay groaning on his back. She grabbed her shoulder bag and threw the baton into it. Then she went over to where Machota lay. He was bleeding from where she had hit him in the head. She grabbed him by the shirtfront and got him into an upright position.

"Listen to me," she hissed in his ear. "There are armed men in the house. You have to help me. Can you get to your feet?"

"Bitch," he groaned in reply.

"You want to die here? It's up to you."

Machota gritted his teeth, rolled to one side, and, with Jean's help, he lifted himself painfully to his feet. "Oh, God," he gasped. "God."

He leaned against her, pulling up his pants. She twisted around, spotted a shadow, and fired two more shots. There was a scream of pain.

With Machota draped around her, Jean stepped past the two bodies in the front entrance and moved out into the drive. There was no sign of anyone.

Jean said, "Where are the keys to the vehicle?"

"In my pocket," he said. She leaned him against the G-wagon and rummaged in his pockets until she found the key. Then she got him in the passenger side and went around and got behind the wheel.

She started the engine, threw the vehicle into reverse, screeched out of the driveway, onto the street, desperately trying to remember how they had come in here, wondering how they were ever going to get out. Beside her, Machota stirred. His bleeding was worse, and he had gone bone white. She had to get him to a doctor. "Hold on, sergeant," she said.

His head lolled around. His eyes flickered a bit. "You don't know where the hell you're going," he mumbled.

"That's why you've got to help me," she said. "Otherwise, we're both dead."

Machota didn't answer. She stole a glance at him. He appeared unconscious.

She sped past the guard post that marked the entrance to the upscale neighborhood, except that now the post was empty. No wonder the armed men could get into the house, she thought.

As she re-entered Kandahar proper, the streets grew darker, traffic sparse. Drab concrete buildings closed in. Jean pulled the G-wagon over to the side of the road and fished out her cellphone, hoping to get a signal. Not much of one.

"Get out!"

She looked up from her cellphone. Machota had regained consciousness. He had the gun she should have taken from him.

"Get the hell out," he repeated.

"Don't," was all she had a chance to say before he shot her.

The force of the bullet slammed into her side and knocked her against the driver's door. In a daze, the light seeping away, she could see him reaching over, unlatching the door. The next thing she was airborne, light as a feather, floating—for about three seconds.

She landed hard on pavement, pain a hot poker digging into her side. She lay on the roadway as the G-wagon sped away.

Then, silence.

She tried to sit up, but it hurt too much to move.

She had no idea how long she lay there. The fight was not to assess the passage of time; the fight was to stay conscious. It was a fight she felt herself beginning to lose. Then a shadow materialized into a figure walking toward her. The figure was holding a gun. No big deal, she thought to herself.

Everyone in Kandahar had a gun.

1

The dream, the recurring dream—not so much a dream as an endless replaying of events—was interrupted when Jean's brother shook her awake.

"How would you like to give me a hand?" Bryce Whitlock said.

"What time is it?"

"Just after five A.M."

"What's up?"

"The Halton police called. They have a body up on the escarpment they need picked up."

"What's a body doing up on the escarpment?"

Bryce shrugged. "They didn't say."

"Like old times," she said, easing herself into a sitting position, rubbing sleep from her eyes.

"Yes," he said. "Meet you downstairs in a couple of minutes."

By the time she dressed, Bryce had the van running and ready to go. As Jean left the house, dawn was a suggestion in the sky over the distant hump of the escarpment. The air was clear and cool. Jean got in beside her brother, and he started forward. "I don't suppose there's time for a coffee."

"They were anxious for us to get up there."

So no coffee until after they made the pickup. The police rotated these calls for body pickups among area funeral homes. This morning, apparently, Bryce's number had come up. They did this basically as a favor to the police. In a few cases, the funeral home ended up taking care of the deceased, but otherwise there was no real money—just a courtesy and early mornings with no coffee.

Bryce yawned as he swung the van west on Main Street, all but deserted at this time of the morning. Milton was the fastest-growing town in the country, but you would never know it now, Jean mused. The fastest-growing population was tucked into bed.

"What time did you get in last night?" Jean asked Bryce.

"Not too late," Bryce replied.

No explaining where he had been or what he was up to. But that was Bryce. Maybe he had a girlfriend. Or maybe not. Intimate brother-sister communication had never been their strong suit.

West on Main Street, the van took the first exit off the roundabout onto Tremaine and then another left onto Fourteen Side Road where the skeletons forming mazes of new home construction were becoming visible in the predawn light. A billboard let the world know that this was yet another DEL CAULDER HOME DEVELOPMENT. A smiling young couple stood in front of a sprawling suburban fantasyland. Happiness was being created here, a whole new world grown up since Jean had left, a world chewing up what once had been farmland.

On Appleby the road climbed steeply toward the escarpment. By now, light streaked the sky. The day beginning to intrude. Jean preferred the night and lots of sleep. That way she didn't have to think about things—like the fact that she was a forty-year-old woman without a job returned to the town where she was born, wondering what she was going to do with the rest of her life.

Things like that.

The van's headlights illuminated the gatehouse entrance to Rattlesnake Point. Bryce navigated the van along a dirt track into a parking lot drenched in light from portable lamps, jammed with police and emergency vehicles. A knot of officers broke apart as Bryce pulled to a stop. Two of them came over as Jean and Bryce emerged.

"Hey, folks," one of the officers said.

"We're from the funeral home," Bryce said. "They called us about a body."

The officers traded glances. The older one of the two said, "Okay, just follow the pathway beyond the parking lot; you'll see where everyone is. It's not far."

"Thanks," Bryce said.

Jean turned in the direction the officer had indicated and saw more light through the trees. "Here we go," Bryce said, turning toward the lights.

As they stepped onto the path, another police officer waved a flashlight at them. "We're from the funeral home," Bryce said.

The officer nodded and said, "See Sergeant Dann over there."

They went along further, toward what Jean imagined was the cliff edge, although in the dark it was hard to see beyond the radiance of the portable lights set up at intervals. The trees surrounding a clearing stood in sharp relief. Under the glare of the lights, Jean could see a staircase leading down the side of the cliff. Mickey Dann was just coming up to the top of the stairs.

Mickey Dann, Jean thought. Well, as I live and breathe. He registered surprise when he saw her, and then tried to hide it with a smile. He was still handsome, Jean thought, a little more rugged-looking than when they dated in high school, and his hair had receded, but it was still mostly dark brown. What's more, he had kept himself trim and in shape.

"I didn't know you were with Halton police," Jean said.

Mickey said, "When did you get back to town?"

"A week ago," she said.

Mickey looked at Bryce. "And this guy's already got you working?"

"I'm a slave driver," Bryce said, without smiling.

"Well, we're all set for you," Mickey said.

"Where is the body?" Bryce said.

"The bottom of the gorge over here, not far from the stairs so she won't be difficult to access, but it's not pretty."

"A female?" Jean said.

Mickey nodded. "I'm afraid so."

"Any idea what happened?"

"What do you need from the van?" Mickey, avoiding her question. "Let me give you a hand."

"Appreciate that," Bryce said.

Daylight worked its way through the clouds as they returned to the van. Bryce went to the rear, opened the doors, and yanked out the stretcher he kept for these occasions. Together with Mickey Dann, they carried it back to the clearing. The stairway was wide, dropping to a landing, and then descending from there to the ground. The K2 eighteen-hundred-watt crime-scene lights positioned at the bottom of the gorge were pointed upward, illuminating the cliff face.

The wind and rain had worked to cut a chimney of rock away from the cliff. The body, or what was left of it, lay at the bottom of the opening created by the rock chimney, crushed among lichen-covered boulders, caught in a circle of light so bright it practically seared the eyes.

Around the lighted perimeter stood another group of police officers—Jean never lost her sense of incredulity at the numbers of police who managed to find themselves at crime scenes with nothing to do except stand around chatting. The group grew silent at their appearance.

Bryce stopped. Jean looked at him. Her brother's face had gone pale. The body was in bad shape, but he had seen plenty worse. They were a family of funeral directors, after all. Their grandfather had started the funeral business in Milton. Their father had taken over from his father. And now, following their dad's death, Bryce ran the business. They had grown up with dead bodies in the fine old Tara-like structure next door to the wood-frame cottage that was home, built in the late 1800s, originally a church, the first in Milton.

Jean stepped forward for a closer look. The dead woman lay on her back, a shattered doll with matchstick arms and legs thrust at odd angles. She was dressed in a dark blue track suit, her head twisted at a grotesque angle. Jagged bone shards had torn through the fabric of her clothing.

"I'm going back to the van for a body pouch," Bryce said.

"You didn't bring it with you?"

Bryce just stared at her. Jean said, "Bring me some surgical gloves, will you?"

He nodded and then clambered back up the stairs, leaving Jean to wonder what was the matter with him. This wasn't like the uber-efficient Bryce of old. She tried to keep her eyes off the mess of the body. She was relieved when Mickey Dann came over to where she was standing.

"Are you back for good?" he asked.

"I'm back," Jean said. "I don't know about 'for good.'"

"You caused quite a stir," Mickey Dann said.

"Did I?"

"It was in all the papers. I saw you interviewed on the CBC."

Jean didn't know how to respond to that, so she said, "Have you identified the body?"

Mickey smiled. "Are you asking as a cop or as an undertaker?"

"Just trying to make conversation, Mickey."

"At the moment, she's a Jane Doe."

"How did you find her? You must have got out here in the middle of the night."

"Around one thirty," Mickey said. "Someone phoned it in."

"Anonymous?"

"Now you are starting to sound more like an investigator."

"Not me," Jean said with a fleeting smile. "Curious, though. Someone found a body at Rattlesnake Point at that time of night. What were they doing up here?"

"Could be kids. We used to come up here, remember that?"

"I didn't but lots of my friends did."

"That's right. You were goody-two-shoes in high school."

Jean chose to ignore that. "You think she jumped off the cliff?"

"What do you think, Jean?"

"Could be suicide. If I were a police investigator, I would certainly consider that possibility."

"But you're not any longer, are you?"

"Of course," she said. "I would also have to consider the possibility that someone pushed her."

"Yeah, you would," Mickey said.

Then she noticed Bryce standing rigid just outside the penumbra of light, clutching the body pouch as he stared at the corpse.

Jean crossed to him. "Are you all right?"

That brought him out of his reverie. "Let's get this over with," he said.

He handed her the surgical gloves she had requested. Once they had struggled into the gloves, they spread out the pouch as best they could beside the body. Bryce stopped, his eyes fixed again on the mangled corpse.

"Bryce," she said.

He appeared to take a deep breath, as if forcing himself to do something he had in fact done dozens of times before. He bent down and grabbed the body, holding onto the fabric of the woman's clothing. Bones cracked and shifted as Bryce strained to turn the body onto its side.

As soon as he accomplished this, Jean, just as she had done many times, pushed the edge of the open pouch as far beneath the body as she could get it.

For the first time she could see the broken, disfigured face of the woman, all but unrecognizable. She did not want to think about the trauma of the woman's body striking these rocks, what she might have been thinking the instant before she hit the ground and life was wrenched out of her—if she'd had a chance to think anything.

When Jean had finished positioning the pouch, Bryce rolled the body back again so that it lay on the pouch and he threw the flap across the body and then adroitly closed the pouch and zipped it up. As soon as that was done, Bryce called to Mickey Dann.

He came over with a yellow plastic strap lock. He pushed the strap through the zipper and then wound it back into the lock, sealing the bag.

"That's it," he said.

"We're going to need some help lifting it up and onto a stretcher," Bryce said.

Mickey whistled at a couple of uniformed officers. When he got their attention, he waved them over.

That's when the girl appeared. Jean saw her first, a lovely, pouty-lipped teenager with dark hair and large eyes against pale, smudged skin. She seemed to materialize out of the morning air. Jean had the impression of everyone standing still in shock, gaping at her.

Jean went over to the girl. She wore a T-shirt and jeans, fourteen, maybe fifteen years old. There were smears of blood on her cheeks and forehead. She was shivering, her arms crossed as though hugging herself to keep warm.

Jean said to her, "Are you all right?"

The girl just stared, her dark eyes filling with fear.

2

The figure knelt down to Jean. Thin moonlight illuminated the grim street and revealed the lined and weary face of Major Shaar Zorn of the Afghan National Police.

"How bad?" he said.

"Feels like my insides are on fire," she managed to say.

Behind Zorn, Jean was aware of two more police vehicles arriving, their headlights framing the street in contrasting light and shadow. Zorn peered down at the wound in her side, interested, but not, apparently, particularly alarmed. Gunshot victims in Kandahar were, after all, a dime a dozen.

"You were not supposed to be there," Zorn said.

"No, I wasn't," Jean said.

"Sergeant Machota said he wanted to borrow my house for a few hours this evening. I thought he was going to use the place to bring a prostitute."

"Did you send those men?"

Jean could hear the squawk of a police radio as Zorn considered the question. He shrugged. "Life in Kandahar is very dangerous. Gunmen can appear anywhere, shooting anyone. Who can say where they come from?"

A team of emergency medical workers now appeared. Zorn said, "I'm sorry this happened to you, Jean. I like you very much. You have been a great help to us."

"Unlike Sergeant Machota?"

Zorn's lined face allowed a slight smile. "We have had our issues with Sergeant Machota. So, apparently, have you."

The emergency medical providers, young and stern-faced, hovered expectantly. As soon as Zorn nodded, the workers in their white coats descended around Jean like falling angels. Someone spoke in Pashtu to Major Zorn. He replied and then said to Jean, "They will take care of you, Jean. You are going to be all right."

Jean wondered.

———————

By the time they turned onto the Queen Elizabeth Way toward Hamilton, the sky had lightened, but any hope of sunshine was lost in a thick gray cloud cover. Bryce spoke for the first time since they left Rattlesnake Point. "Didn't you and Mickey Dann date in high school?"

"We went out a couple of times, that's all," Jean said.

"What does that mean?"

"It means we went out a couple of times."

Bryce resumed his silence. Jean longed to stop for coffee but when they transported a body from a possible homicide, there was no stopping until they reached the hospital and turned the corpse over to the regional coroner's office. Just to make sure they didn't, their van was accompanied by a patrol car.

Jean thought of the girl back at Rattlesnake Point. One of the female officers present had wrapped a blanket around her and taken her away, while Mickey Dann fumed, and demanded to know how twenty-five police officers who supposedly had fanned out to search the area had failed to spot her.

As for the kid herself, she wasn't talking; at least she wasn't while Jean and Bryce were present. Police had found no identification on her person, and it wasn't certain whether she was connected to the dead woman. If there was a connection, then what were the two of them doing at Rattlesnake Point, and how did they get there since no vehicles had been found in the park area?

"What do you think happened back there?" Jean said.

"I learned not to ask those questions a long time ago," Bryce said. "I just pick up the bodies. Better that way."

As the van approached the separate garage entrance for the coroner's office at the Hamilton General Hospital, Bryce was on the phone, letting the staff on duty know that he was delivering a body. The corrugated iron door started up a moment later, and the van drove through. Inside, two attendants waited beside a gurney as the van came to a stop. The attendants helped Bryce transfer the body pouch onto the gurney. One of the attendants checked to make sure the yellow seal was intact.

By now the following police car had also pulled into the garage. The two uniformed officers got out, and then everyone followed the attendants as they pushed the gurney through two sets of double doors into the morgue. The morgue attendant on duty had the paperwork ready, and Bryce quickly signed the forms verifying the time and the date they delivered Jane Doe.

Ten minutes later they were in the van again, headed back to Milton. The sun finally managed to poke through the clouds as they turned back onto the Queen Elizabeth Way. Jean felt suddenly very tired. Bryce looked stoic behind the wheel, concentrating on the thickening eastbound rush hour traffic. Rush hour, what a misnomer that was, Jean mused. These days it was rush *hours*. All rush hours, all the time—and not a whole lot of rushing.

"You must be dead," she said to her brother.

He grinned and cast a sidelong glance in her direction. "Statements like that encourage a lot of bad undertaker jokes."

She laughed. "Okay. But aren't you tired?"

"Put it this way, it will be good to get home."

"Have you got anything on for today?"

"A viewing tonight at seven. What about you?"

"A shower when we get back, and then I'll go over to Mom."

"Listen," he said. "There's something you should know."

"Okay."

Bryce kept his eyes firmly on the road. "That woman this morning."

"The woman at Rattlesnake Point."

"I know her."

Jean blinked in surprise. "What do you mean, 'you know her?'"

"I know her. I know who she is." He paused before he added, "Her name is Shawna Simpson. We've been—I don't know, I guess you'd have to say we've been dating."

"Why didn't you say something to the police?"

He shrugged. "At first, I wasn't sure it was her, and then when I realized who she was, I was in shock, and then the girl showed up . . ." He allowed his voice to trail off.

"Do you know who the teenage girl is?"

Bryce shook his head.

"You arrive at a crime scene, you know the identity of the Jane Doe, and you don't say anything. The police aren't going to like that one bit."

Bryce kept his eyes fixed on the road and didn't say anything.

"As soon as we get home, you should call Mickey Dann," Jean continued. "Tell him you weren't certain who the victim was before you got her body to Hamilton. Then you took another look and now you think it may be someone you know."

When Bryce still didn't say anything, Jean said, "Did you hear me?"

"I heard you," he said.

They drove the rest of the way home in silence.

3

"You always wanted us to talk more, Mom," Jean said. "You thought I was too closed, too private. Well, here we are talking because you're the only person I can talk to, the only person who would understand what I'm feeling right now.

"So if you would like to know how I'm feeling, I'm feeling like crap," Jean continued. "I'm back in the town where I don't want to be, and I've lost the job I wanted more than any other. How did I manage to do it? How did I screw up so badly? I ask myself that a lot. It's all a blur. One day I'm a proud member of something that I've wanted to be part of since I was a kid, a pretty darned good member, too, if I say so myself, and then, suddenly, it's over, and it's like I was never there. I'm not even acknowledged. How did that happen?"

Ida Whitlock did not respond. She stared at the ceiling of the hospice room on the second floor of the Milton District Hospital. Ida had been in this room for the past three weeks, ever since she had suffered a stroke after being diagnosed with the cancer that had seeped into her bones and was inoperable. A matter of time, the doctors had gently told Jean and Bryce. Ida's impending death, the need to be with her mother as she came to the end, had brought Jean back to Milton. Otherwise, she was not certain she ever would have returned.

But here she was, sitting at her mother's bedside, the late morning light streaming through the windows, softly illuminating a plain, comfortable room in a small town hospital, an anonymous place to die. Jean thought yet again of the irony: all your life you acquire things, get to know things, and then you die in a place unknown to you, surrounded by nothing familiar.

Ida abruptly twitched on the bed, turning restlessly, her small body rigid, then relaxed. The nurses said it was the medication causing these reactions. But Jean wondered if her mother was having nightmares, the jerking motions of her body being their physical expressions.

Jean rose from the chair and sat on the edge of the bed, trying to hold her mother's frail body; a body that grew smaller each day, it seemed to Jean, a body melting away, like the Wicked Witch in *The Wizard of Oz*. Except there was nothing wicked or witchlike about her mother; just a tiny woman dying.

Ida's eyes sprang open, and she cried out.

"Mom, it's all right," Jean said. "I'm here."

She called out again. Something that sounded like, "garlock."

Jean leaned closer to her mother's anguished face. "What?"

"Garlock," Ida repeated. "Garlock. Garlock!"

Then her words became unintelligible again. After that, Ida settled and resumed her blank gazing at the ceiling.

"That's happened before." One of Ida's caregivers, a small Asian woman named Achala, had entered the room.

"Mom moving around like this, you mean?"

Achala nodded as she adjusted the bed covers. "And calling out like that. 'Garlock.' Always that same word. Any idea what it means?"

"I don't think it means anything," Jean said.

"Or it means everything—she keeps repeating it, so I think it must somehow be important to her."

"I don't know," Jean said.

"The secrets of our parents," Achala said.

"Somehow, it's hard to imagine Mom with secrets," Jean said. "But I guess you never know."

"That's the thing, right? We never really know." Achala shrugged and smiled. "Call me if you need anything else," she said.

"Yes, thank you."

Achala slipped out of the room, leaving Jean alone with her mother. She leaned forward and kissed Ida's damp forehead. "Do you keep secrets, Mom?" Jean asked aloud.

Of course, Jean thought, stroking her mom's cheek. We all keep secrets. The daughters certainly do. Why not the mothers?

Garlock.

Dead tired at mid-morning, feeling she had done her duty to her mother for the time being at least, Jean only wanted to get home, have something to eat and maybe even indulge in the previously unheard luxury of a nap.

She took the stairs to the ground floor, and then went along the corridor to the lobby. It was deserted except for the tall, well-dressed man with smooth brown skin and dark hair artfully silvered at the temples. As he turned to her, Jean thought vaguely that he could be a male model, what with that smile showcasing teeth so white they practically glowed.

"Ms. Whitlock?" the man said.

When Jean nodded, the man extended a slim hand—manicured, she noticed—and said, "I'm Ajey Jadu."

She looked at him blankly. His smile widened. "You don't know me, but my sister is married to Del Caulder. I guess your Mom and Del went to school together."

"Yes, sure," Jean said. "How is Del?"

"Hey, Del is Del, right? He won't be satisfied until he's built every house in the province. I'm working with him to make sure that happens."

"Good for you," was all Jean could think of to say.

"I recognized you from the papers. I guess your mom's here, right?"

"Yes," Jean said.

"My dad, Om Jadu, he's in here, too. His heart."

"I'm sorry to hear that."

They both fell into an awkward silence. Ajey gave her another of his bright, toothy grins. She wondered how anyone got their teeth that white. "Well, I just wanted to say hello," he said.

"I hope you're father's going to be all right."

Ajey shrugged and a look of sadness crossed his handsome face. "We don't know about that," he said. "All you can do is hope. Take it day to day."

"Yes," Jean agreed.

Jean's cellphone buzzed in her jeans pocket. "I'd better take this," Jean said. "I've been waiting for a call from my mother's doctor."

Now why did she say that? she wondered. What was the point of the white lie? Maybe because there was something oddly discomfiting about Ajey Jadu. Was he too handsome? Or too close to Del Caulder, not exactly a family friend, although she had tried hard to stay out of her family's various feuds.

"Good to finally meet you, Jean," Ajey said. "Probably see you around."

Jean nodded. They shook hands again as she got her phone out. She recognized the number on the screen and groaned inwardly. But she answered the call.

"Jean, it's Grace over at the mayor's office."

Jean looked around to make sure that Ajey Jadu was gone before she said, "Grace, yes, how are you?"

"I didn't know you were back in town until this morning," Grace said.

"You know, Mom," as though that explained everything.

"I know, sweetie, and I'm so sorry. The mayor's pretty broken up, I can tell you."

Grace paused to allow Jean to say something. But Jean didn't respond. Finally, Grace said, "He wants to see you. Are you free for lunch?"

She was going to have to confront her uncle at some point. Might as well shake off her fatigue and get it over with rather than try to draw it out by ducking him.

She said, "Yes, I suppose so."

"He said to tell you, 'the usual place.'"

"Yes," she said. "The usual place."

4

When Jean was growing up, Uncle Jock Whitlock would occasionally take her to lunch in the park fronting the old town hall.

The park hadn't changed much, Jean reflected after she left the car at the funeral home and then strolled over. The memorial to the town's First World War fallen was still there, of course, and so was the bandstand, although it looked as though it had been refurbished. A new, much more modern municipal building had been added to the fortress-like town hall with its imposing stone façade. She didn't much like the new addition.

She found Jock Whitlock already seated on the bench facing away from the old town hall. His hair was grayer than she remembered, so was his mustache, and it looked as though he had put on weight. He held up a brown paper bag as she seated herself beside him.

"I got you tuna on rye, the way you used to like it," Jock said.

"I can't remember the last time I had a tuna sandwich," Jean said.

"Probably the last time you had lunch with me."

He fished into the bag and handed her a sandwich wrapped in wax paper and a Diet Coke. Jock watched her unwrap the sandwich.

"We finally got into the new house last week," he said.

"A new house for a new wife," Jean said.

"Not so new. Desiree and I have been married for a couple of years now."

"Where did you end up building?"

"Out on Derry Road. Come out and visit us."

"Sure," Jean said noncommittally.

"You're looking good, Jean. You lost some weight, right?"

"About twenty pounds," Jean said.

"The same amount I've put on," Jock said. "It's being out nights. You end up eating crap."

"You should go to the gym," Jean said.

"Gym? Who has time for a gym? Twenty years ago, this job was a breeze. I could finish town business in the morning and then manage the dealership in the afternoon. But those days are long gone, let me tell you. Twenty-four-seven. That's what this job is now."

"Come on, Jock, you've been complaining about the job since I was a kid. You love it."

"I'm not so sure about that, the way this town is growing, the development, all the crap you have to put up with. I'm getting too old for it."

Jock opened his sandwich. "Shoot. I asked for pastrami on whole wheat. They've given me pastrami on rye." He looked at Jean. "Gives you some idea how little influence I have over events around here."

He studied the sandwich for a couple of beats before he said, "The Mounties are bastards. I love cops, but not those guys. They are pompous, bureaucratic pricks who will protect their asses no matter what. They're more than happy to throw someone like you under the bus."

"It's finished now," Jean said. "Whatever I may think at this point, it's over, and it's time to get on with my life."

"So are you back for good?"

"I don't know," Jean said. "We'll see how it goes with Mom. After that, I'll decide what I'm going to do."

"How's Ida doing?"

"Why don't you go over to the hospital and find out for yourself?"

Jock held his pastrami sandwich in his hand as if it were an offence against nature. "I can't bring myself to do it. I don't want to see her like that. I guess I want to remember her the way she was."

Jock laid the sandwich atop the paper bag he had spread out on the bench, as if the effort to eat it had become too much.

"You know I loved your mother," he said in a matter-of-fact voice.

"That's what Dad always used to say," Jean said. "But I never knew how serious he was."

"I was the one who dated her first. Her family moved here from Montreal. I asked her out, and made the mistake of introducing her to your father. The next thing . . ." Jock shrugged. "Well, he always was Lucky Ned Whitlock, wasn't he?"

"Was he?"

"That's what we used to call him, Lucky Ned. So Ida fell in love with Lucky Ned, not with his younger brother. There you go. That's life. But I don't think I ever stopped loving her. I certainly tried over the years, but I never stopped."

"I didn't know any of this," Jean said.

"That's because I never told anyone, not even your father, although he guessed—and certainly not your mother. I just sat there quietly over the years, played the good brother-in-law, kept my mouth shut, my feelings to myself. But I always loved her."

"Why are you telling me this, Jock?"

"Because Ida is dying, I suppose, and I want you to know why I don't go to see her."

"Does 'garlock' mean anything to you?"

Jock looked at her. "Why should it?"

"Mom keeps calling out what sounds like garlock. Her caregivers have noticed it, too."

"Doesn't mean anything to me," Jock said. He picked up the sandwich again, and nibbled at it tentatively. "You want your Diet Coke?"

"Thanks," Jean said. He picked up the can, snapped the cap before handing it to her. "I hear you were up on the escarpment this morning."

Now it was Jean's turn to look at him. "How did you hear that?"

"Hey, I'm the mayor, remember? I hear everything. Especially when the police find a body up there." He paused to take a bigger bite out of the sandwich. "Do they know who it is?"

Jean thought of what Bryce told her. Aloud she said, "She went over to Hamilton as a Jane Doe."

"So no identification?"

"Not so far as I know," Jean said. "Why don't you ask Mickey Dann?"

"He's got the case? Your old boyfriend?"

"He's not an old boyfriend," Jean insisted. "We dated a few times, that's all."

"I thought he was a boyfriend."

"Since when did you take so much interest in my teenage love life?"

"Since it occurred to me you might have had one."

"When did that happen? A couple of weeks ago?"

Jock shrugged. "It's taken me awhile to come to terms with the fact that you're no longer my little niece eating tuna fish sandwiches with her uncle."

"Believe me," Jean said, "Mickey Dann played no part in the transition."

Jock looked disappointedly at his sandwich before picking up the bag and placing what was left of it inside. "I'd better be getting back."

"Why do I feel like I'm missing something here, Jock?"

He was on his feet, holding the bag, so to speak. "What would that be?"

"The reason why you called me?"

He grinned. "Maybe I just wanted to have a sandwich with my niece and welcome her back to town."

"Maybe," Jean said. "But it's never that simple with you."

"You haven't touched your sandwich."

"Maybe I don't like tuna so much anymore."

"I'll keep that in mind," Jock said.

"Incidentally, I met someone who works for Del Caulder this morning."

"Yeah?"

"Ajey Jadu. Apparently, he's the brother of Del's wife."

"I know Ajey. His sister's about half Del's age."

"You and Del with your trophy wives."

"Desiree isn't that much younger."

"Fourteen years?" Jean said.

"That's not so much," Jock said.

Jean noted the defensive tone in her uncle's voice before she said, "I hadn't realized Del remarried."

"Dumped his wife about three years ago. His kids are ready to kill him."

"What about your kids, Jock?"

"Tessa and Dan understand the situation. They know what I've been through."

"It's good that they're so understanding," Jean said, fighting to keep the irony out of her voice.

"Besides, Dan is working in California, and Tessa's playing hippy with some guy on Vancouver Island."

"Far away from the madding crowd," Jean said.

"How did you run into Ajey?"

"He approached me at the hospital," Jean said. "Apparently his father is there."

Jock said, "Del's got Ajey on the payroll while he tries to convince council to let him develop the escarpment."

"What's he want to do with the escarpment?"

"What else? He wants to build houses up there. High-end stuff."

"You're kidding. Can he do that?"

"We'll see."

"You and Del never did see eye to eye."

"He's responsible for three quarters of the new development around here, and good on him, I suppose. He's made himself a very rich man. I never thought he'd ever learn to tie his shoe laces."

"The escarpment is a little out of your jurisdiction, isn't it?"

"Nothing around here is out of my jurisdiction. This is my town. Del's going to have to deal with that."

"Come on, you mean to tell me you don't like all this development," Jean said.

"I like it just fine. I only wish he wasn't responsible for it, that's all."

"The clash of the titans," Jean said.

"Watch out for Ajey," Jock said. "I don't think that bastard ever does anything by accident."

"What? You think he arranged to meet me this morning?"

"That thing about Ida," Jock said.

"What thing?"

"People say things when they are pumped full of painkillers. But they don't mean anything."

And that's when she wondered: if it didn't mean something, why say anything?

5

The deceased was a longtime local resident named Elmer Cole. Elmer had died of natural causes early that morning at Oakville Memorial Hospital.

Now his mortal remains were laid out on the embalming table in the basement of the funeral home. As Bryce stripped away the hospital gown and removed a wristwatch and wedding band from the dead man, his mind wandered to the woman on the escarpment. He mustn't think about her, not right now.

He busied himself massaging Elmer Cole's muscles and limbs to relieve the rigor mortis, already regretting that he had told Jean that he knew the dead woman. A moment of weakness. Jean wouldn't say anything, he concluded as he went about using disinfectant to carefully wash the body from head to foot.

Or would she?

She was a cop, after all; his sister, yes, and therefore loyal, but still a cop and honest as they come. That was Jean's problem with the Mounties. Why she now found herself out of a job—she was too damned honest for her own good.

So he should not have said anything to her. But he had. He had said he would call Detective Mickey Dann. But he hadn't. He was putting off that phone call. Jean had her own problems with which to deal; his relationship with a dead woman was the least of them.

Jean's tangle with that Mountie sergeant who was her superior in Afghanistan was a mistake, no question. Not that Bryce blamed her. But Jean was an attractive woman and men had been hitting on her since the two of them were in high school together. She had left a trail of broken hearts around Milton. There was a time, if he remembered correctly, when Jean actually liked all the male attention. That didn't excuse her boss, didn't excuse what had happened.

Bryce forced himself to refocus. Concentrate on Elmer Cole, dead and gone Elmer. A man in his eighties who had been ill for some time before drifting off into—what?

Well, nothing as far as Bryce was concerned. Dust to dust. No more than that. But wherever Elmer was headed, whatever his destination, Bryce would do his level best to make his remains presentable for Elmer's survivors on this earth.

Particularly the deceased's eyes and mouth. They were all-important. The eyes must look natural in order to reassure grieving relatives that their loved one was at peace. The eyes of the dead tended to sink into their sockets, and so to counteract that, he placed plastic caps on the pupils, and then closed the lids over them before applying a dab of cream to avoid dehydration.

Next, the mouth. Bryce used a curved needle threaded with suture string to sew the jaw shut—making sure not to sew it too tight so that the mouth retained its natural line and Elmer didn't look as though he was grimacing unhappily in death.

As he worked, Bryce's cellphone began to vibrate. The sound made him jump. Good grief, he was nervous this morning. What was the matter with him? Well, he knew, didn't he? But he wasn't going to think about that right now. He wasn't going to think about her lying crumpled and broken among the rocks at Rattlesnake Point.

So he ignored the vibrating phone and began the process of removing the blood from the body, making an incision into a neck vein and inserting a drain tube.

Bryce made another incision into the groin area where he inserted a second tube that would pump two gallons of formaldehyde and water through the veins, replacing the blood. When that was completed, he used a trocar to puncture the stomach and start draining fluids from internal organs in the abdomen and thoracic cavity. That way the gas and urine still in Elmer's body would not break down the organs and cause them to decompose, a process that could begin with alarming speed and spread through the body, causing it to turn green and stink to high heaven, the equivalent for the dead of flesh-eating disease—the undertaker's nightmare.

Not today, though, Bryce thought as he injected the formaldehyde into the torso that would protect Elmer's body. He packed the anus with cotton gauze to ensure there was no unsightly seepage.

He once again washed the body to rid it of any chemical residue. The family had provided a freshly-cleaned suit for Elmer, a dark blue garment with an old-fashioned double-breasted jacket, shiny from years of wear.

Despite all the modern gadgetry designed to make the funeral director's job easier, you still had to use muscle and patience when it came to dressing a corpse—wrestling with legs and arms to get clothes onto an unresponsive body. If there remained a Keystone Kops moment in the preparation of the dead, this was it; nothing at all elegant about it, Bryce mused, having spent a lifetime attempting to find a better way. No, this was the slapstick comedy part of the process; luckily no one saw it.

However, modern technology had come to the rescue of the funeral director's back when it came to lifting bodies. After he had wrestled Elmer Cole into his blue suit, Bryce used a mortuary lift, an electronic moving device that ran along a track above the embalming table. He worked nylon straps beneath the body and then hooked them to straps hanging from the lift. He pressed a button on the control panel, and Elmer lifted off the table. Bryce guided him to the nearby open casket and lowered him inside.

Elmer finally at rest.

A job well done, Bryce decided, surveying his pale handiwork. This was the job he had been doing all his life; the job his father, Ned, had done before him, and his grandfather before that. A family of undertakers long in the business of making death palpable for the living, providing comfort to those left behind by ensuring the departed were sent on their way with appropriate dignity. Only Jean and his Uncle Jock had rejected the family business. It was too late for Jock, of course, but now that Jean was back, well, he could use help, no doubt about it. He would talk to her about that. But later.

Once this business on the escarpment was resolved.

———

At five o'clock, members of Elmer's extended family—his two daughters and their husbands and three grown kids—arrived at the funeral home to pay their respects. Everyone had a good cry, and after they left, Bryce, aided by Doris Stamper, his assistant director, put the casket lid in place and wheeled Elmer into the main viewing room.

There was a visitation from seven till nine. Doris, her heavy body encased in black, greeted visitors at the door. Not many people showed up, and those who did were old and bent and solemn, as if aware that they were soon headed in the same direction as their friend.

By the time the last regrets had been murmured, final memories shared, it was nearly nine thirty. Bryce left Doris to lock up and walked over to the house. Jean had dinner waiting, a nice surprise. "Having you home has its benefits," Bryce said.

"That's reassuring," Jean said. "Maybe you won't throw me out on the street, after all."

"Well, not tonight, anyway," Bryce said.

Dinner was nothing fancy, a roast chicken, accompanied by Basmati rice and a tossed salad. But it was certainly better than the bowl of oatmeal he usually had at this time of night, standing at the kitchen sink. He asked Jean if she wanted any wine, and she shook her head. He decided to pass as well. They sat together at the tiny table in the kitchen, eating in silence.

"This is good," he said. "What's that on the salad? A balsamic dressing?"

Jean nodded and put her fork down. "Did you call Mickey Dann?"

Bryce kept his eyes on his plate. "Didn't have time. Had to get a body ready for tonight's visitation."

When Jean didn't say anything, he glanced up at her. He found her staring at him. "What?" he said.

"I can't believe you know who that woman is and didn't call," Jean said.

"They will identify her soon enough," Bryce said. "They don't need me."

"Bryce, this is a potential murder investigation. You can't just ignore it."

"I said I knew her," Bryce said. "I didn't say we were living together or anything. What? You think I killed her?"

"It's not what I think. It's what the police are going to say the longer you delay."

"If they haven't identified her by tomorrow, I'll call Mickey Dann."

Bryce watched Jean push uneasily at her chicken. He swallowed a mouthful of salad and said, "How was Mom today?"

"Restless," Jean said. "She kept mumbling a word. Has she done that when you're there?"

Bryce shook his head. "What kind of word?"

"I think it was something like 'garlock'. Does that mean anything to you?"

"I don't think she's in any state to be saying anything meaningful."

"So it doesn't mean anything?"

"Not to me it doesn't."

"It didn't mean anything to Jock, either," Jean said.

That surprised Bryce. "Jock was at the hospital?"

"No, we had lunch together."

"What did he want?"

"Just to have lunch, he said."

"It was something," Bryce said, unable to keep the anger out of his voice. "With that bastard, it's always something."

"Bastard's a little strong," Jean said.

"Okay, he's not a bastard—he's Jock. Amounts to about the same thing."

"He was telling me he's built a new house."

"The new house. The young wife. Del Caulder's developments popping up everywhere."

Jean looked at him. "What's that supposed to mean?"

"Uncle Jock has acquired all the bells and whistles, hasn't he?"

"What? Thanks to Del Caulder?"

"They're thick as thieves."

"That's not what Jock says."

"Now I hear Del wants to build up on the escarpment."

"Jock says he's not happy about that."

"Well, we'll see," Bryce said. He raised and lowered his eyebrows suggestively.

When they finished their meal, Jean helped Bryce clean up. He joked that it was like old times. She laughed and said, "I don't seem to remember the part about you helping clean up."

"It just goes to show what's happened to your memory," he said.

She rinsed the plates and put them in the dishwasher. Then she straightened, took a deep breath, and said, "Bryce do you have an alibi for last night?"

Bryce looked at her in surprise. "A what?"

"An alibi? Can you tell the police where you were last night?"

"I'm not going to need an alibi—am I?"

"I'm just asking. Do you have one? Is there someone who can verify where you were last night?"

"Don't worry about it," Bryce said.

"That's not an answer," Jean said

"I'll handle it."

That wasn't an answer, either. But she didn't say anything.

6

Staff Sergeant Adam Machota barked: "What is your name Corporal?"

"Corporal Jean Whitlock, sir!" came the reply.

"And what is your mission here with IPOB?"

"To train and mentor members of the Afghan police, specifically in the area of major crime—sir!"

"And what is your other duty here, Corporal?"

"I'm not certain what you're getting at—sir!"

"You know what I'm talking about, Corporal."

"Yes, sir, to fuck you, sir, and not complain about it."

Staff Sergeant Adam Machota grinned, a liquid smile sliding languorously across his handsome face; a supremely confident smile, the smile of a man who knew what he wanted and was certain he would get it. The staff sergeant began stripping off his clothes. Jean turned and ran. He called after her, "Repeat to me what your mission is here, Corporal!"

Jean was outside, racing through the narrow streets and alleyways of Kandahar City.

She encountered a group of young Afghan men, the senior police officers she had been working with for the past six months to improve their investigative skills. She begged them for help. Machota was after her. She could not escape. The young men just laughed and began to close in. She turned into another alley that became narrower and narrower as she ran along. Finally, she reached a high stone wall blocking her way. She turned as the men descended upon her laughing uproariously, tearing at her clothes.

Machota appeared, pushing through the crowd, naked, that spreading grin arrogantly in place. "What is your role here in Afghanistan, Corporal? Tell me what it is. Tell me!"

And then she was awake. Sitting up, gasping for breath. Early morning sunlight streamed in the window. She got out of bed, still breathing hard, wondering if Bryce had heard her—probably thinking she was crazy, suffering from Post-Traumatic Stress Syndrome or something.

Maybe she was, for all she knew.

She went to the window with its view of the funeral home and the adjacent parking lot just as Bryce appeared. He wore jeans and an open-collared shirt, looking pressed and formal even when he was trying for casual. But that was Bryce. If anyone was born to be an undertaker, it was Bryce Whitlock. What was she born to be? she wondered as she watched her brother. Apparently, it wasn't to be a police officer. Maybe just a scared, middle-aged woman shaking off bad dreams.

No, she determined as she stripped off her pajamas. There was more to her life than that. But what? Caregiver to a dying mother? Yes, that was her role for the time being. Everything else was beside the point. Coming from a family whose job it was to guide the living into the undiscovered country that was death, she should be able to do that.

Shouldn't she?

As she entered the tiny shower stall in the guest bathroom, she thought again about Bryce and the fact he had not told the police about his involvement with the woman on the escarpment. His reluctance to tell the police what he knew was worrying. She thought about phoning Mickey Dann herself.

But as soon as she thought of it, Jean dismissed that idea. She was not about to create problems for her brother. She was no longer a police officer; this was not her job. Her job was to take care of her mother.

And to figure out what she was going to do with the rest of her life.

————————

Jean got to the hospital, bought a coffee from the Tim Horton's outlet in the cafeteria, and then took the stairs to her mother's second floor room. She found Ida lying quietly, draped in sunlight.

"Good morning, Mom," she said, seating herself beside the bed. "I didn't bring you coffee. I didn't think you would want it."

Ida stared at the ceiling. Jean removed the plastic lid from her steaming cup and sipped at it.

"How did you sleep last night? I slept okay, I suppose. Except I dreamed of Adam Machota again. I'm not supposed to dream about him. I'm not supposed to let him get to me. That's what I tell myself, but it doesn't seem to be working out. At least it didn't last night."

She drank some more coffee. "I haven't told you about Adam, have I? I suppose I didn't want to worry you. I thought I could handle things myself, but it turned out, I couldn't. The sergeant is not the sort of individual that you can handle easily. How do you handle a homicidal sociopath? How did I allow myself to end up in a compromising situation that I was never going to be able to explain my way out of? Well, I've paid the price. A bad night's sleep is the least of it, Mom. The least of it."

A tear rolled down Jean's cheek. She wiped at it angrily. "Shit," she said. And then, "Sorry, Mom. I should watch my language around you."

"Good morning." Achala, her mother's caregiver, entered the room. "Your mom had a very peaceful night."

"So she's been telling me," Jean said.

Achala looked at her and then smiled. "Yes, of course. But you know, she has been talking to us, to me and the other nurses."

"Garlock," Jean said.

"Other words, too," Achala said. "The doctors think we are all crazy. They say it's impossible. That your mother couldn't be saying anything at this stage."

"Well, I heard her," Jean said. "Unless we're all losing it."

"No, look at this," Achala said, withdrawing a folded piece of notepaper from the pocket of her smock. "Just for fun, a few of us put together a list or words we've heard your mother say. None of the words make sense, at least to us. Maybe they will mean something to you."

Achala handed the paper to Jean who unfolded it. There were five words printed in block letters:

GARLOCK
FARGO
RATTLESNAKE
NIGHT
MURDER

Jean looked up from the sheet. "Murder? You're sure about that?"

"I did not hear her say it, but one of the other nurses on duty swears she did, so we wrote it down. Do these words mean anything to you?"

"No," said Jean. "I've asked my brother and my uncle about 'garlock'. It doesn't mean anything to either of them—and I can't imagine my mother had anything to do with murder."

"Like I said, it's one of the other nurses. She probably didn't hear her right."

7

"You have a visitor," Doris Stamper said when Bryce came into the funeral home late in the morning.

"Couldn't you handle it?" Bryce was always amazed at the inability of anyone but him to take responsibility.

"She insisted on seeing you," Doris said.

A tall woman in a short red dress sat in one of the wing-backed chairs in the main reception area. Black hair was pulled back into a bun to emphasize high cheekbones and the angular lines of her face. A handsome woman in red, Bryce thought fleetingly as he shook the woman's hand. "I'm Bryce Whitlock," he said. "Sorry, I hope you haven't had to wait too long."

"Mandy Dragan," the woman said. "I probably should have phoned for an appointment."

Bryce seated himself in a nearby chair, allowing his face to settle into the look of attentive concern adopted for clients. "Ms. Dragan, how can I help you?"

"A close friend has died," the woman said. "I wanted to talk to someone about funeral arrangements."

"You would be handling the arrangements?" Bryce said.

"I think so, yes."

"The deceased had no family?"

"Not that I know of," Mandy Dragan said.

"Are you the executor of the deceased's estate, by any chance?"

"I wouldn't think so, no. I'm not sure about any of the details. All I know is that Shawna is dead and there is no one else to take care of her."

"Shawna?"

"Shawna Simpson."

Bryce fought to keep the surprise off his face. He said, "Then the police have officially identified her?"

"I suppose they have. The police were there when I arrived at Shawna's apartment. That's how I know what happened to her."

"She had been missing?"

Mandy shrugged. "I don't know about missing. I hadn't heard from her for a couple of days, and she wasn't answering her phone, so I went around to check on her."

"Did the police send you here?"

"That's right. I got a call from a Detective Dann this morning saying that the autopsy had been completed, and the body could be released. I didn't know what to do, whether anyone would even claim the body. This detective suggested I talk to you."

"I see," Bryce said.

Mandy said, "Is there a problem?"

"No, not really," Bryce said hurriedly. "It's just that if there are family members surviving the deceased, they ordinarily have the say when it comes to funeral arrangements."

"There are no family members as far as I know. Her parents died a couple of years ago, and she was an only child."

"No aunts or uncles or cousins?"

"I don't think so," she said.

"You would have to sign an affidavit to that effect," Bryce said.

"I guess that would be fine."

"Okay, we'll take down some particulars from you, and then we will get in touch with Hamilton General where I believe they have the body."

"That's what the police said, yes."

"If Hamilton General says it's all right to release the body, then we will go ahead and bring Shawna back here. Do you have any idea what you would want to do after that? Burial? Cremation?"

Mandy faltered and Bryce saw the air of self-confidence she had exuded until now begin to falter. "I don't know, I really don't. That cop, he suggested I come here so—"

"It's all right." Bryce adopted the soothing voice required for these occasions. "You don't have to make any decisions right now.

We'll get Shawna back, make certain there are no other relatives, and then we can proceed from there. How's that?"

Mandy looked relieved. "Sure. That's fine."

"Let me get a couple of the forms you need to fill out."

He was about to rise when she said, "You're not nearly the bastard Shawna said you were."

"I beg your pardon?"

"Shawna was attracted to you, but she thought you were a cold bastard." She flashed him a quick smile. "Her words, not mine."

Bryce managed to say, "I'm not sure I know what you're talking about."

The smile turned icy. "You know exactly what I'm talking about. What are you saying? You weren't sleeping with Shawna?"

Bryce just looked at her, speechless.

Mandy stood. "I've left my card there on the side table."

Bryce leaned over and picked it up. "You work for Del Caulder," he said after looking at the card.

"Doesn't everyone in this town, one way or another?"

"I don't," Bryce said.

"Get Shawna's body from Hamilton, and then call me, and we will go from there."

"Yes, we'll certainly do that," Bryce said, trying to regain his professional composure.

"It was good to finally meet you, Bryce. I must say, I'd heard a lot about you from Shawna."

"I'm sorry about your loss." Bryce couldn't think of anything else to say.

"Are you?" She raised and lowered dubious eyebrows. "I wonder about that."

She turned and was walking away toward the main entrance before Bryce rallied enough to call after her. "Ms. Dragan."

She turned to him. He got out of the chair and came over to her. "Do you mind if I ask…"

"Yes?"

"What did you tell the police?"

"For the moment, you don't have to worry about the police," Mandy said. "But you do have to be concerned about me."

"How is that?"

"As soon as you have the body, call me," Mandy said.

He couldn't help but notice the movement of her hips beneath the dress as she went out the door.

8

Before the cancer overwhelmed her, Ida had occupied an apartment in a modern complex around the corner from the funeral home so she would be close to Bryce.

Jean used her key to unlock the front door. She crossed the living room to open curtains and admit the afternoon sunlight. Jean told herself that she wasn't really snooping into her mother's life, that it was all right to be here, that her mother was at the end, and at some point soon everything in here would have to be searched through and discarded anyway, so why not start now?

Except today Jean was searching out the secrets of her mother's life, prying into areas her mother would never have wanted her to poke around in.

Or would she?

Perhaps Ida's mumbled words were no more than that, meaningless, just like Jock said. Perhaps her daughter was making something out of nothing, a bored former police officer with nothing better to do than create a mystery that wasn't there.

Still …

Jean pulled the piece of notepaper from her pocket, unfolded it and laid it out on the kitchen table. Again, she studied the printed words.

GARLOCK
FARGO
RATTLESNAKE
NIGHT
MURDER

She turned from the paper and gazed around, still surprised by the place where her mother had decided to move once she gave up the house on Thomas Street. If that house had become too big for Ida, this apartment seemed too small; a woman's life reduced to a tiny microcosm of itself, evidence of the futility of material goods. At the end, the *things* you cherished would be mostly thrown away. What was the point of it all?

What was the point of anything? she thought.

The original furniture in the old Thomas Street house, heavy, dark pieces that declared prosperity in the Whitlock household, had been replaced by the sort of anonymously modern stuff you acquired in one of those big box furniture warehouses. Was Bryce's hand behind this? She thought he had better taste—or her mother had better taste.

A massive mahogany armoire, the single piece rescued from Thomas Street, dominated the apartment's north wall. If there were secrets, it was possible they were housed inside this hunk of furniture where what survived of her mother's past was stored. The armoire was fitted with doors and drawers, topped with the wooden soldiers in tall hats and red coats Ida had collected for some reason, their cheeks a bright crimson to denote rosy good health, their mouths permanently arranged in rictus grins, forever happy warriors.

She opened the ornately carved doors at the center and moved a glass box containing pieces of her mother's jewelry. A photo of her mother, still quite lovely in middle age, smiled out from the middle shelf.

Smaller doors were embedded in the bottom of the armoire. Opening those, Jean found two yellow plastic storage cases. The first case contained personal papers, including her father's death certificate—a stroke when Jean was sixteen. She had been sitting at the kitchen table watching Ned on the phone—ironically, speaking to his doctor—when he was stricken suddenly, dropping the phone and collapsing to the floor. He was dead by the time the ambulance arrived. Or when the ambulance must have arrived. She could remember vividly the moment the stroke hit, the look on her father's face, but nothing else, certainly not the arrival of the paramedics or the events that followed. All of that had been lost.

She found a white envelope containing five black and white prints, yellowing around the white borders. Ida posed with a young man Jean did not recognize. The young man was tanned and blond, the embodiment of the handsome high school jock, the youthful Robert Redford type, maybe a little softer, less hard-bodied than Redford in his heyday, but definitely in that wheelhouse.

In three of the photographs Ida and the blond kid posed, arms loosely around each other, grinning happily at the camera. In a fourth photo, the blond boy appeared to be trying to tickle a retreating, laughing Ida. In the fifth photograph, their lips were touching. Not a deep, passionate kiss, more like something you would do when you are horsing around for the camera.

Jean put the photos aside and began searching through the cabinet, rediscovering her mother's past, things she knew and things that surprised her. For instance, after Ned's death Ida had applied to teach in Saudi Arabia. What would she have done with a teenaged boy and girl? Jean wondered. Could she and Bryce have accompanied her? Not that it made any difference; there was no sign her application had gone anywhere.

What the cabinet did not yield was the key that might unlock the mumbled words of a dying woman. There was only the Robert Redford-like boy posing with Ida. Was his name Garlock? Or Fargo? Or Fargo Garlock? Did someone murder Fargo Garlock—or maybe Garlock Fargo— one night up on Rattlesnake Point? If that was the case, then the mystery was solved, wasn't it? Awfully easy, Jean thought as she gathered up the envelope containing the prints and shoved them into her shoulder bag. Too easy. Nothing involving the past, let alone murder, was so simple. And did she really believe her mother was once mixed up in such a crime?

Hard to imagine. No, not hard to imagine. Impossible.

9

This is crazy," Bryce said later that evening as they finished dinner, and Jean told him about her visit to their mother's apartment.

Jean handed him the word list that the hospital caregivers had compiled. "What am I supposed to make of this?" Bryce said after he scanned it.

"I heard Mom say 'garlock' myself. I told you about that."

"So what?"

"The nurses heard it too. They've also identified other words."

Bryce said, "I've been with her a hundred times, and she's never said anything."

"Well, I heard her," Jean maintained. "And I have no reason to believe the nurses are lying."

"You're all imagining things. Like finding pictures in clouds. She's dying, pumped full of painkillers, in and out of consciousness, nothing she manages to say is going to make any sense."

"Or maybe it does make sense. Maybe she's trying to tell us something."

Bryce looked at her for a long moment before he said, "Jean, I can't believe what I'm hearing. You're an experienced police officer. You should know better."

"I'm also a daughter who is losing her mother," she shot back. "I just want to stay open to the notion that as she leaves, she may be trying to get a message to us."

Jean sat back, swallowing, fighting to keep her temper in check. Bryce looked contrite. "Look, I'm sorry," he said. "I know there is a lot of emotion here. On a number of levels."

"Isn't there for you, too? Or is everything so bottled up?"

"That's unfair. Nothing's bottled up. It's just that you and I have different ways of expressing things, that's all."

Jean got up from the table and went over to her shoulder bag. She retrieved the envelope containing the photographs and came back and handed them to Bryce. He looked at her questioningly.

"I found these in the cabinet at Mom's apartment.

Bryce took the photos out of the envelope.

"This kid with the blond hair?" Bryce was laying out the photos on the table in front of him.

"Any idea who he is?" Jean asked.

"Haven't a clue. What? You think there's some connection to these so-called messages Mom is attempting to leave us?"

"I don't know," Jean said. "But I've never seen these photos before, and neither have you."

"I suspect when we go through Mom's things we're going to find lots of stuff we either didn't know about or have long since forgotten. She had a whole life before we came along. This guy, he could have been a boyfriend, a neighbor. Who knows? He looks harmless enough."

Jean rose, collecting their plates. "Hey, let me get those," Bryce said.

"It's all right, I'm up. Did you speak to Mickey Dann today?"

"That's what I wanted to talk to you about," Bryce said.

"What's that mean?" Jean left the dishes in the sink and then came back to the table and sat down.

"They've identified Shawna," he said.

"Mickey told you?"

Bryce shook his head. "A woman came to the funeral home today, a friend of Shawna's, she said. She wanted to make arrangements for her."

"You're kidding," Jean said. "Who is the friend?"

"The name won't mean anything to you. Mandy Dragan."

"Do you know her?"

"No, but she knows me. She knows that I was involved with Shawna."

"How would she know that?"

Bryce shrugged. "Shawna must have said something to her," Bryce said, then added, "She wants me to pick up the body from Hamilton General."

"The police have released the body?"

"Apparently."

"Why is this Mandy Dragan making the arrangements? Where is Shawna's family?"

"According to Mandy, Shawna has no family."

"Is that true?"

"I don't know. I suppose it could be."

"You mean you were 'involved' with this woman and you never talked about her family, where she comes from, brothers and sisters?"

"It wasn't like that," Bryce said.

"What was it like?"

"Sex," Bryce said. "Not a whole lot of conversation."

Jean rolled her eyes. "Listen, you could be in trouble here."

"Because I had sex with her?" Bryce said testily.

"Because you're withholding information from the police."

"But the police must have decided it's not a homicide. Otherwise, why would they release the body."

"Just because they've released the body doesn't mean they've decided anything," Jean said.

"I'm going to get the body from Hamilton General. Whatever this Mandy Dragan does or does not do, Shawna at least deserves to be properly taken care of."

"I don't think you should go near that body, not until you talk to the police."

"Do me a favor, will you?"

"What's that?"

"Nose around a bit, see what you can find out about Mandy Dragan."

Jean looked at him. "You're beginning to scare me."

"You were a criminal investigator, training people in Afghanistan to do this stuff. That means you must have been pretty good at your job."

Jean sat back in her chair as if to get a better look at her brother. "Are you in trouble, Bryce?"

He placed Mandy Dragan's card on the table in front of Jean. "That's what I'm hoping you can find out."

10

Bryce drove to Hamilton first thing the next morning to pick up Shawna Simpson's body from the coroner. He had debated about sending one of his associates but then steeled himself and decided he would go. That way nothing would seem out of place; everything done as it was normally done.

Business as usual.

Even so, he felt unusually tense as he drove into the garage at Hamilton General. He took deep breaths and forced himself to stay calm. If the police had connected him to Shawna he would have heard about it by now. They would not be waiting behind the doors of the morgue to pounce on him. They were releasing the body. They most likely had decided her death was not a homicide.

Most likely.

And sure enough, there were no waiting cops. The pouch containing the body was ready to go. The tag attached to the sealed zipper confirmed that the police had in fact identified her: Shawna Simpson. They had a Burlington address he didn't recognize. He signed the usual forms and one of the attendants handed him the death certificate. Two attendants transferred the body to a gurney and wheeled it out to Bryce's van. Moments later, he was on his way again.

Business as usual.

He dreaded the next part. The part back in the basement of the funeral home stripping away the body bag, exposing Shawna's white, broken corpse collapsed and twisted on the embalming table. Someone once told him that a body after an autopsy resembled a butchered animal. That description came back again with a force that was like a blow.

A few days ago, Shawna was a gorgeous woman with a lovely body. But this corpse provided scant evidence of beauty. The body had been cut horizontally from shoulder to shoulder, joined at the sternum and then down to the pubic bone in a Y shape to enable removal of the organs. Once the coroner had finished, the torso had been loosely sewn back together.

To remove Shawna's brain, an incision had been made at the back of the skull, cutting across from ear to ear so that the scalp could be peeled forward. After the removal of the brain, the skull had been carelessly stitched back together, giving Shawna's head a freakish Frankenstein's monster appearance. The brain along with the other organs had been placed in a plastic bag and inserted into a body cavity.

Good God, he thought. Can I do this?

His mind drifted to the night he met Shawna at the bar in Toronto's fashionable Yorkville district where he had stopped for a drink with a friend, Pete Adler, in town from Los Angeles. Shawna had walked in, tall and statuesque, commanding in a place already filled with spectacular women. Pete, the perpetual ladies' man despite his recent engagement, immediately hit on her.

But it wasn't Pete Shawna was interested in. She wasn't even put off by the fact that Bryce was an undertaker operating his family's funeral business in a town west of Toronto. She worked out in that area herself for a developer named Del Caulder. Did Bryce know him? Of course, Bryce said. Everyone knew Del. His father had grown up with him. His father and mother attended high school with Del.

That intrigued her—or appeared to intrigue. With Shawna it was hard to tell. From the beginning, she played the role of the enigmatic beauty superbly, present and accounted for but always elusive. Giving away just enough personal information to keep it interesting. But always seeming to hold something back. Bryce told himself he didn't care; if playing the mystery woman was her thing, that was fine with him. He didn't care.

Or did he?

He cared now. Most embalmers would not go near a loved one. Instead, they would bring in another funeral director to do the work. He had heard of instances where someone in the business worked on a mother or a wife, but that was rare, and now Bryce knew why.

The thought of touching Shawna's body, trying to make something out of this mess in front of him, made him nauseous. He couldn't do it. He would have to, but not right now. Right now, he needed some air and time to think.

Bryce stumbled upstairs as the front door of the funeral home opened and a large man entered. His long brown hair, thinning at the crown, was pulled back into a pony tail. The man seemed somewhat surprised to find himself alone inside a funeral home. Bryce straightened around, took a deep breath, and called out, "Hello, can I help you?"

The man blinked a couple of times as Bryce came toward him. His unexpected visitor possessed the girth of a wrestler or what Bryce thought could be a wrestler. The size of him added to the air of menace. Bryce had the uncomfortable impression that he was confronting a tough guy.

"I'm looking for Bryce Whitlock," the man said.

"I'm Bryce," he said, and then added formally: "How can I help you?"

"Want to talk about funeral arrangements."

"Certainly," Bryce said. "May I get your name?"

"Dave Mackie," the man said and held out a big hand.

Bryce took it and said, "Mr. Mackie, why don't we sit over here?"

He led Dave Mackie into one of the sitting rooms. Dave Mackie looked uneasy, as if he expected corpses to be spread around the room. Bryce offered him the same chair as Mandy Dragan had occupied, and then seated himself across from him. "I know this is a difficult time, so we'll try to make the process as comfortable for you as we can."

"Appreciate that," Dave Mackie said.

"First of all, let's get the name of the deceased."

"It's Shawna," Mackie said. "Shawna Simpson."

11

There were two of them, both inspectors, Walter Duke, a bullet-headed, sharp-featured prairie dog with two pieces of black coal for eyes; Jill Lowry, a heavyset grandmother type with a smile like a blessing you would never have known was an RCMP officer if it weren't for her uniform.

The two inspectors were already seated when Jean entered the interrogation room. Formal pleasantries were exchanged. Inspector Lowry wanted to know how Jean was doing. Would she like some water before they got started? Jean declined. Inspector Duke rustled papers around and cleared his throat. "You have previously stated, Corporal Whitlock, that Sergeant Adam Machota lured you to the house occupied by Major Shaar Zorn of the Afghan National Police, and once there sexually assaulted you, is that correct?"

"I don't know that he lured me," Jean replied. "He said that Major Zorn had invited us to his house to thank us for our help during the past seven months."

"But Major Zorn wasn't there, is that what you're saying?"

"That was the case, yes."

Inspector Duke continued: "It was after the two of you entered that you say Sergeant Machota attempted to rape you."

"Yes, as I've stated before, he struck me several times and then tore at my clothing."

"And you fended him off, is that it?"

"I was able to engage my police baton."

Inspector Duke looked down at the papers in front of him. "I understand you are quite proficient with the baton, Corporal. Something of a master of the weapon, I understand."

"I don't know about that," Jean said. "But I was able to stop the sergeant's attack."

"And at that point the house was invaded by armed men?"

"Yes."

"And you employed your service revolver to shoot at least two of the intruders, and then you helped Sergeant Machota to the G-wagon and drove out of there. That's your story?"

"That's what happened," Jean said.

"At which time, Sergeant Machota shot you and then drove off, leaving you lying on the street."

"That's correct."

Then it was Inspector Lowry's turn. She blessed her first question with a smile. "You understand, don't you, Corporal, that Sergeant Machado has a different version of these events?"

"I understand that he is not telling the truth," Jean said.

Inspector Lowry was undeterred. "According to the sergeant, you went to Major Zorn's house. When the two of you entered, the major was not there. He says that no sexual assault took place, that no sooner had you arrived than you were attacked by the armed men. You panicked, but Sergeant Machota was able to open fire, killing several of the attackers. However, one of his bullets must have ricocheted and hit you in the side. He helped you out of the house, got you into the G-wagon, fending off more attackers, and then was able to get you safely to hospital."

Inspector Lowry looked up from the pages she had been reading from. Her eyebrows rose questioningly.

"Obviously, I dispute most of that," Jean said. "There certainly was 'a sexual assault,' as you call it. Sergeant Machota shot me and then left me on the street. If Major Zorn hadn't happened along, I would be dead."

Inspector Duke joined in. "What we are looking for at this point, Corporal, is evidence that would corroborate your version of these events."

"I suppose you could ask yourselves why I would put my career in jeopardy by making these claims if they weren't true."

"Is that what you think, Corporal?" Inspector Duke asked. "That you're putting your career in jeopardy?"

"Am I not?"

"Sergeant Machota says he is shocked by the claims that you're making," Inspector Duke said. "All he can think is that you are embarrassed by your actions during the attack, and are trying to cover them up with these claims."

"That's preposterous," Jean said.

"Is it?" countered Inspector Duke. His rugged face was the picture of institutional blankness, and all the more accusatory for it.

"I understand what you are saying, Corporal Whitlock." Inspector Lowry weighing in with one of her blessing smiles. "But we still need proof that goes beyond the he-said-she-said aspects of this situation."

"Major Zorn was there," Jean said. "He would be able to verify what happened."

"Major Zorn has disappeared, as you know." Duke made it sound as though Jean might be responsible for the major's disappearance. "The Afghan police have issued a warrant for his arrest. It's suspected that Major Zorn may have orchestrated the attack in question."

"Yes, that's what I told the investigators," Jean said. "He thought Sergeant Machota was coming alone. I believe he planned to have him assassinated."

"Why would he do that?" The gentle grandmother voice of Inspector Lowry.

"I'm not sure," Jean answered. "But something happened between them."

Inspector Lowry cleared her throat and arranged to look slightly embarrassed before she said, "Sergeant Machota has told us he believes you and Major Zorn were having an affair."

"What?" Jean had not heard this before.

"Is this true, Corporal?" Inspector Duke joining in.

"It is most certainly not true," Jean said emphatically.

"Sergeant Machota has testified that Major Zorn tried to have him killed because he was jealous of Machota's relationship with you."

Jean spoke carefully, trying to keep the anger out of her voice. "Sergeant Machota and I had no relationship beyond the fact that he was my superior officer, and I reported to him."

"What about Major Zorn?" Duke asked.

"I mentored Major Zorn for close to seven months," Jean answered. "We had a good, professional relationship. No more than that."

"He had no romantic interest in you?"

Jean may have hesitated a moment too long before she said, "No, not as far as I know."

Inspector Lowry pounced on that, no longer the grandmother. "As far as you know. But unbeknownst to you, there could have been some romantic interest that might have encouraged him to orchestrate the attempted murder of Sergeant Machota."

"I don't know," Jean said uneasily. "I suppose it's possible. But it's hard to believe. I was leaving the country in a couple of days. So was Sergeant Machota."

"All the more reason why he might have wanted to take action against Sergeant Machota," Inspector Lowry said. "He couldn't bear to see the two of you going off together."

"Even if that were true," Jean said, "it still doesn't excuse Sergeant Machota's actions."

"Unless what happened between the two of you was consensual," Inspector Lowry's voice had hardened. The grandmother had left the room. "Unless you are making up this story in order to excuse *your* behavior that night."

Jean swallowed the bile she felt rising in her throat. "Let me reiterate," she stated, fighting to keep her voice even. "Sergeant Machota asked Major Zorn if he could use his house that night. Then he lied to me and said Major Zorn had invited us back. When we arrived, Sergeant Machota attacked me, tried to choke me, struck me several times, ripped my blouse and bra. I fought him off with my police baton. When I finished with him, he was bleeding and bruised. Surely that must have shown up in the reports."

"Sergeant Machota says he sustained those injuries engaging with your attackers."

Jean shook her head. "The sergeant was only semi-conscious when I got him out of there and into the G-wagon. I drove him to safety."

"Despite what you say he'd done to you."

"Yes, of course. No matter what had happened between us, a fellow officer was in trouble. I wasn't going to leave him behind."

"And you say he repaid your professionalism by shooting you." Did she hear just the hint of sympathy in Inspector Lowry's voice?

"That's what happened. Those are the facts."

Silence filled the room. It would be easier, Jean decided, to decipher the side of a cliff than read the faces of her interrogators.

12

What was she doing? What she shouldn't be doing. Letting her mind drift back into dark places where it must not linger—back to the past she promised not to think about.

She forced herself to refocus. She was sitting in the parking lot of a mall on Dundas Street in Oakville, keeping an eye on the Caulder Homes condominium office. That's what she was doing. That's what she should be concentrating on.

By why was she sitting here like this? Protecting her brother? That was the rationale, wasn't it? That was always the rationale with Bryce when they were growing up. He was the older brother in years but in actual fact she was the big sister, more mature, grounded.

Bryce was the needy kid, demanding attention. Bryce sucked all the air out of the room while Jean played the quiet, studious, reliable sister. If she said she would do something, she did it. If she said she would meet you, she was there—and on time. The good girl. The smart girl. The tough girl—always standing up for her brother, protecting him from the world.

So here she was protecting him again. But protecting him from what? Jean tried not to think about what the answer to that question might entail. His refusal to tell police what he knew about Shawna Simpson disturbed her. Was he hiding something? His involvement in her death? She did not want to think about that, either. Instead, she focused on the entrance to the mall office complex where, according to Mandy Dragan's business card, she worked as a "consultant" for Caulder Homes.

Across the street, one of the double glass doors at the entrance to the condominium office opened and a tall woman strolled out. Jean consulted the business card. It showed a tiny color photograph of an austere Mandy Dragan, her dark hair pulled back to emphasize the business professional. The Mandy who now crossed the parking lot allowed her hair to flow loosely to her shoulders, a much more sensual-looking woman than her photo implied.

As she approached a Jaguar she aimed a transponder key at it and a moment later was behind the wheel starting the ignition.

Jean followed the Jag as it turned onto Dundas Street, headed west. When she got to Bronte Road, Mandy turned north, until she reached Derry Road where she made a left. Wherever she was going, Jean mused, she was trying to get there in a hurry, pushing the Jag to over eighty kilometers an hour.

The Jag slowed when it reached the intersection of Bronte Street South and Main, made a left, and then, abruptly, another left onto a dirt road to a construction site adjacent to a two story brick house stranded among big yellow earth-moving machines.

Jean decided not to risk following Mandy onto the site. Instead, she parked across the road from it and got out. She opened her shoulder bag and removed the palm-sized surveillance binoculars she carried, and raised them to her eyes.

Through the lenses, Mandy jumped into sharp focus crossing to the brick house. A figure in a hard hat emerged and walked toward Mandy. She stopped and allowed the figure in the hard hat to approach. The figure removed the hard hat and embraced Mandy. She put her arms around him and gave him a brief kiss on the mouth.

The man she kissed was South Asian, handsome even at this distance. Two good-looking people embracing on a muddy construction site. A nearby sign announced that someday soon this would be Escarpment Heights, the latest condominium project from Caulder Homes. She realized with a start that she had met the handsome man at the hospital—Ajey Jadu, Del Caulder's brother in law. Jean watched as Mandy followed Ajey into the house.

Jean lowered the binoculars and turned back to the car as another vehicle pulled up behind it. Detective Mickey Dann was at the wheel.

13

Bryce tried to keep his voice neutral as he said, "You are handling funeral arrangements for Shawna Simpson."

"That's right," Dave Mackie said.

"Are you related to the deceased?"

"Friend," Mackie said.

"Usually, we require a family member to make arrangements," Bryce said.

"I was kind of like a big brother in her life."

"If you're not a family member, Mr. Mackie, I'm afraid there's not much I can do. At this point, funeral arrangements are already underway."

That caused Dave Mackie's face to harden perceptibly. "You don't understand, *I'm* making the arrangements."

Bryce kept his voice at the calm, professional level he adopted when confronting difficult clients. "In cases where two parties insist on overseeing funeral arrangements, we suggest either the parties meet—"

"I'm not meeting anyone," Mackie said. His voice had become a snarl.

"Or you get a lawyer and he works out some sort of compromise."

Dave Mackie leaned forward, his body tense and somehow threatening. Bryce had the distinct feeling the room had gotten smaller. "I'm not going to say this again," Mackie stated. "I'm taking care of the arrangements. I don't care who else is involved. You tell them to get lost. I'm dealing with this."

"I'm not in a position to do that," Bryce said.

"You goddamn well get yourself into a position," Mackie said.

Bryce took a deep breath and said, "Mr. Mackie you can't come in here and start threatening. That's not going to work."

"Yes, it is," Mackie said. "It's going to work fine because you're going to do what I tell you to do."

Bryce stood and said, "If you continue to threaten me like this, I'm going to call the police."

Mackie remained seated but he raised his dark eyes to Bryce and that made him seem all the more threatening. "Yeah, why don't you do that, why don't you call the police? While you're on the phone with them, you mention how you knew Shawna, how the two of you had this weird love-hate thing going, how you were with her the night she disappeared. Make sure you tell them all that when you call, okay?"

Bryce tried not to show the sense of alarm he was feeling. He managed to say, "I don't know what you're talking about."

Dave Mackie sat back in his chair, making a throwaway gesture with his hand. "Don't you? Then call the cops."

Bryce took another deep breath and said, "Let's lower the temperature a little bit, shall we?"

"Sure, let's do that. Let's agree that I'm handling the funeral arrangements."

"For the moment, no one can handle the arrangements because the police haven't released the body," he lied. "As soon as they do, why don't I get in touch with you?"

Mackie stood and faced Bryce. He was actually shorter but within the curiously diminishing confines of the room, he loomed much larger. "When do you expect that to happen?" he said.

"It all depends how backed up they are at the morgue in Hamilton," Bryce said smoothly, feeling on firmer ground now. "A day or two in all likelihood."

Mackie reached into his back pocket and pulled out a worn leather billfold. From it he extracted a dog-eared card. He handed it to Bryce. The card read, "David Mackie, Automotive Products." There was a Milton address and phone number.

"As soon as you get the body, call me at this number."

"I'll do that," Bryce said.

"I know you will." Dave Mackie smiled for the first time since he had arrived at the funeral home. It was not a nice smile.

"Car trouble?" Mickey Dann said, getting out of his vehicle.

"I thought I heard a funny sound, so I pulled over," Jean said, dropping the binoculars back into her shoulder bag.

Mickey nodded toward the Caulder construction site. "Looking for a new home?"

"I could be," Jean said.

"You could just drive in there," Mickey said. "You don't have to look at it through binoculars."

Jean smiled. "I didn't want condo sales people jumping all over me."

Mickey nodded and said, "I was going to give you a call."

"Yeah? What were you going to say when you called me?"

"I thought maybe we could get together for coffee or a drink."

"Two old high school pals catching up?"

It was Mickey's turn to smile. "How about two world-weary cops?"

"Sure, why not?" Jean looked at her watch. "You could buy me a coffee now if you have time."

"There's a Tim Horton's over on Steeles Avenue."

"How about the Starbucks on Martin Street?"

Mickey laughed and shook his head. "Just don't tell any of my Tim Horton's friends. Fifteen minutes?"

"See you there," Jean said. As she returned to her car, she glanced across the road at the brick house all but lost amid the tangle of construction machinery. Mandy Dragan's Jag was visible in front.

As she drove away, Jean wondered about the chances of an accidental encounter with Mickey Dann. Maybe she had been involved in police work too long, but when it came to human behavior, chance was low on her list of possibilities. Better to believe Mickey wanted something. That way she could be pleasantly surprised when he didn't.

The Maplehurst Correctional Complex was directly across the street from the Starbucks. Jean swung into the parking lot, passed the service station and parked in front. No sign of Mickey as she got out of the car.

Inside, at this time of day, the place was almost empty. Mickey arrived five minutes later. Not a bad looking guy, she thought as he walked in. She tried to imagine him back in high school and couldn't. Adulthood had erased any signs of the teenager she once dated. Or maybe she had simply wiped most of the details of those years off her memory map. She had hated that time, couldn't wait to get out of Milton and put everything behind her, including high school dates.

Mickey smiled when he saw her. Nice smile, she thought. Idly, she wondered if he was a drinker. He didn't look like one, and that was certainly to the good. He could use some help in the clothing department, but he was a cop and cops were by definition lousy dressers.

"Been waiting long?" Mickey said.

She shook her head. "What are you having?"

"Coffee black. Here, let me get it."

She stepped to the counter. "It's on me."

"Hey, you're the one unemployed."

The teenage girl behind the counter issued a professional grin ruined by dead, disinterested eyes.

"How may I help you?" she asked.

"Regular coffee. And I'll have a strawberry smoothie." She handed the girl a twenty dollar bill. "And don't let him pay."

"I guess you're pretty determined, huh?" Mickey said.

"Yes, I am," Jean said, accepting her change from the teenager.

"I'll try to keep that in mind."

They sat on either side of a low table, awkward for a moment, Mickey busying himself with the lid of his coffee while Jean inserted a straw into her smoothie.

"That girl up on the escarpment," Jean said.

"The teenage kid," Mickey said.

"Is she okay?"

"She's not talking to anyone. We don't know whether she's mute or if it's some sort of trauma resulting from whatever happened up there."

"Do you know who she is?"

"We don't think she's Shawna Simpson's daughter, but otherwise there was no identification."

"What makes you think she's not the daughter?" Jean said, making a show of moving the straw around in her smoothie.

"We've interviewed several people who knew Shawna. She was forty-two years old. She could have had a daughter, I suppose. But if she did, no one we talked to knew about her."

"Did Shawna work around here?"

Mickey grinned, but his eyes narrowed. "There you go sounding like an investigator again."

She gave him a straight look. "You think there's something to investigate? It's not a suicide?"

Mickey turned his eyes away, the smile still in place, but a little more forced. "She worked in the mayor's office."

Jean looked surprised. "She worked for my uncle?"

"I'm not sure she worked directly for him, but she was in the office."

"Was she from around here?"

"And here I thought we'd be reminiscing about the high school proms we attended together." Mickey's smile was gone.

"We didn't go to the prom together. Did we?"

"You don't remember." Mickey looked offended. Hard to tell if it was real or if he was putting it on.

"I've even got a photograph of the two of us to prove it," Mickey continued. "We were definitely together at our high school prom."

"Oh, God. Don't tell me. I can't imagine how I must look."

"You look great. I look like a hick in a rented tux with dress pants that are too short. I'll show it to you some time."

"Now I'm embarrassed," Jean said.

"Don't be. It was a long time ago."

"Did you ever get married?"

"Briefly. A girl from Acton. Big mistake. Well, that's probably not fair. A mistake. Not a big one. Just a mistake. What about you?"

"Marry?" She shook her head. "No. Career. Dedication. Silly things when you look back on them."

She concentrated on her smoothie. Why did that question always embarrass her? Why did her answer always sound so vapid?

Mickey smiled and said, "The job. Even in Milton, it tends to suck up everything. Not that this town is exactly the singles capital of the world."

"I don't suppose it ever was."

"What about Bryce?" Mickey said. "He never married either, did he?"

"Something about the two of us." Jean trying to make light of it.

"The way I hear it, there is no shortage of women who would like to marry Bryce," Mickey said.

That surprised Jean. "Oh?"

"It's Bryce that doesn't want to marry the women."

That made Jean think Mickey wanted more than just coffee and a little high school nostalgia. She said carefully, "This is not the stuff of brother-sister conversation, at least not with Bryce and me."

Mickey shrugged. "I guess I envy him—if half the stories are true."

"To me, he's just a hard-working funeral director," Jean said. "Right now, we're more concerned with our mother than anything else."

"How's she doing?"

"She's dying, Mickey. I'm back for the end."

"I'm sorry, Jean."

She pasted on a smile that didn't quite work.

14

Jean spent what remained of the afternoon at the hospital with her mother.

Ida lay quietly. No shouted mystery words today, simply an elderly woman dying. Jean sat next to the bed, enjoying the closeness, not saying anything but recognizing the silent, enduring bond between them, the bond that soon was to be broken. But not now, she thought, not today.

She replayed the meeting with Mickey Dann, still not certain whether she had coffee with an old high school beau—for the life of her she could *not* remember that prom night date—or a homicide detective who knew something she didn't and was probing. Probably the old high school beau.

But still.

She remained at the hospital until after eight, leaving only when it had grown dark in the room and she started to doze off in the chair.

When she got home, there was no sign of Bryce. There was leftover chicken in the fridge. She leaned against the counter, munching on a leg. Through the front room window she could see that there was a light on in the funeral home and decided he must be working late.

Jean went outside and crossed to the funeral home. The ground floor was dark, except for a single lamp light in the reception area. She called her brother's name. No answer.

She went downstairs and that's where she found him, in darkness, seated near the embalming table where the mangled corpse of Shawna Simpson was laid out. An open bottle of Scotch stood on the table near Shawna's foot. Glass in his hand, Bryce looked blearily at her as she approached.

"Are you all right?"

"I really screwed everything up," he said, his voice slurring.

"Bryce, you shouldn't be down here like this."

"No, I suppose I shouldn't," he said and took another drink from his glass. "But here I am, feeling sorry for myself."

"Let's go to the house," Jean said. "I'll fix you something to eat."

He waved his glass in the direction of Shawna's body. "I really liked her. You know that? Not love, I don't think. You'd be crazy to fall in love with Shawna, but I liked her. Despite everything, I liked her."

"So you wouldn't harm her," Jean said.

"Is that what you're thinking?"

"I'm not thinking anything, Bryce. I'm asking you."

He sat back, as though contemplating the question. "She drove me crazy, that's for sure."

"Bryce."

"If anything, she's the one who harmed me. Really messed with my head in ways I didn't think possible. Crazy emotions I hadn't felt since I was a kid. But throw her off a cliff?" He shook his head and flashed a weak smile. "I might have been tempted on occasion."

He peered up at his sister and the smile was gone, replaced by dark, worried eyes. "But they're going to think I did, aren't they?"

"I don't know, Bryce, are they?"

He finished what liquid was left in his glass before he said, "Given the circumstances, I suppose."

"Is Mandy Dragan going to help them?"

"Did you see her?"

Instead of answering, Jean said, "What do you know about Ajey Jadu?"

He took a while to consider this before he said quietly, "I know him. What's he got to do with anything?"

"Mandy met with him today."

"They both work for Del Caulder."

"So maybe it's nothing more than that."

He waved his empty glass. "Like I said, I'm screwed."

"No, you're not," she said.

"Easy to say."

"I think you're better than you're making yourself out to be," she said.

"Maybe I've got you fooled."

"Or maybe you're not fooling me at all."

Before he could reach for the Scotch bottle, she plucked it away. "Let's get out of here," she said. "This isn't going to accomplish anything."

He rose unsteadily to his feet. "There's something else," he said.

"What is it, Bryce?"

"A guy named Dave Mackie."

"What about him?"

"He came around today, kind of threatening. He knows about me and Shawna."

Bryce swung around unsteadily to give the corpse of Shawna Simpson a final, doleful look. "I liked her," he said. "I really did." He turned away from the body and gave Jean a blurry look. "There's something I should have told you."

"What's that, Bryce?"

"I was with her."

"With Shawna? When?"

"The night the police found her body on the escarpment."

15

Why did she let him get away like that? Jean wondered the next morning. She should have been tougher with Bryce, forced him to confront what he was doing—and what the hell was he doing, anyway? He had been with Shawna on the last night of her life. He said everything was fine. When he left her around one o'clock in the morning, she was sound asleep. Up till then there had been no indication anything was wrong.

So now here he was belatedly admitting he may have been the last person to see her alive. If there were already two people who knew of his connection with Shawna, it was a matter of time until the police knew it, too.

Bryce was her brother and she would try to protect him, no matter what. But did 'no matter what' include murder? She continued to hope that whatever had happened to Shawna, it was not murder. If it was, that would require a whole other level of covering for her brother.

Could she do that? Well, that was the question, wasn't it? A question she hoped she wouldn't have to confront.

The Bronte Street North address on Dave Mackie's business card turned out to be a garage on a scruffy-looking lot beside the railroad tracks just south of Steeles Avenue. Half a dozen banged-up vehicles were lined up in front of the garage. Jean found a spot for her car at the end of the line and parked there.

The mouth of the garage was a yawning black hole occupied by four tough-looking characters loitering in jeans and greasy coveralls, smoking, taking a lot of surly interest in her. Behind them, inside the dimness of the garage, Jean could make out the outlines of a car up on a hoist. Jean picked out one of the four, a burly guy with an unkempt black beard. She addressed him: "Is Dave around?"

"Inside," the burly guy said, flicking ashes off the butt of the cigarette he held between blackened fingers.

She went past the four into the garage. To her left was a grimy office area behind a chipped and scarred counter. Three men huddled around a desk. They held Tim Horton's coffee cups and jerked up in surprise as Jean came over.

"I'm looking for Dave," she said.

One of the three got up from the desk carrying his coffee cup and came over to the counter saying, "I'm Dave. What can I do for you?"

"I'm having some trouble with my car, I'd like you to look at it," Jean said.

"We don't do that sort of thing," Dave said.

Jean looked at him in surprise. "You're a garage, aren't you?"

"We sell parts for cars," Dave said. "We don't fix 'em."

"Someone said you did repairs."

Dave shrugged. "Someone was wrong."

"That's weird, Shawna told me to get in touch with you."

Dave looked at her. "Shawna?"

"Shawna Simpson."

The men behind Dave had stopped talking and now stared at her.

"She's a friend," Jean went on. "I'm new in town. She said if I needed help I should get in touch with you."

"When were you talking to Shawna?"

"I don't know. A couple of weeks ago, I guess."

"Yeah? How do you know her?"

Jean took a wild stab in the dark: "Ajey introduced us."

"Ajey?"

"Ajey Jadu. You know him?"

Dave visibly relaxed. The suspicion evaporated from his eyes. "Sure, I know Ajey. Are you and Ajey mixed up?"

Jean put on a glittery smile. "Hey, he's okay."

"So he introduced you to Shawna?"

"He thought I could use a friend."

"But you knew Ajey when you got here?"

"From Toronto," Jean said. "He said to call when I got to town. I called."

"Sorry I can't fix your car," Dave said.

"Shawna must have been mistaken," Jean said. She smiled again. "I'll give her hell next time I see her."

"You see Ajey much?"

"Saw him the other day," Jean said, thinking of their encounter at the hospital.

"Next time you see him, tell him I'm trying to get in touch, will you?"

Jean tried another stab in the dark: "About that thing?"

The suspicion once again clouded Dave's eyes. "What thing is that?"

"Must have been something else. I'll have Ajey call you."

"You do that. Sorry about the car."

"That's okay," Jean said. "Maybe I'll see you around."

That produced a thin smile from Dave. "Yeah. Sure. Whatever. It's a small town."

"It sure is," Jean said.

Jean felt three pairs of eyes on her as she left the office. The four guys outside also watched her as she crossed to her car.

Bryce felt like hell. The last thing he remembered with any clarity was Jean finding him drinking Scotch beside Shawna's body. *God*, was that stupid. If anyone else but Jean had seen him like that—he didn't want to think about the consequences. He had to be more careful with his drinking. And what he said to Jean. He vaguely remembered telling her about spending the night with Shawna.

He steeled himself and then went downstairs fearing that he had left the body on the embalming table overnight, time enough for bacteria to get into the organs and start to eat away. But the sickly sweet smell of a decomposing corpse did not assault his nostrils as he entered the embalming room. The body was in the refrigeration unit. Jean must have done it before going to bed. Thank goodness for sisters, he thought. Well, most of the time thank goodness for sisters—except on those occasions when drunken brothers confided too much.

He wheeled Shawna's body out of the refrigeration unit, steeled himself once again before going to work removing the plastic bag full of the organs so he could pump in the formaldehyde solution that would prevent decay. Once that was done, he returned the corpse to refrigeration.

Then he called Mandy Dragan.

"Did you get the body all right?" Mandy asked as soon as she came on the line.

"Yes," he said. "But there's a complication."

"No there isn't, Bryce," she said adamantly. "There is no complication."

"A guy named Dave Mackie showed up yesterday afternoon."

The line went silent for a time. Then Mandy said, "What did he want?"

"He wants to make the funeral arrangements, and he doesn't want to hear someone else got there first."

"What did you tell him?"

"I tried to tell him arrangements were already underway, but he wasn't listening. Dave's not very good at listening from what I can see."

"Dave's an asshole," Mandy said.

"So you know him."

"Listen, just go ahead. One way or another I want what's right for Shawna. I don't care how it's done or who does it, so long as it's done."

"It will get done," Bryce said.

"Must be weird, huh?" Mandy said.

"What do you mean?"

"Working on your lover's body over there at the funeral home. The woman you killed."

"I didn't kill her," Bryce said.

"Well, someone did," Mandy said.

"Is that what the police are saying?"

Silence on the line.

"Mandy? Is that what the police are saying?"

The line went dead.

16

Ida's condition remained unchanged, said the duty nurse in charge when Jean arrived. No surprise. Jean greeted her mother and rearranged her blankets, totally unnecessary, but at least it made Jean feel more like a caregiver, less a helpless daughter sitting there like—what her mother used to say—a bump on a log. She kissed her mother's dry, pale forehead, mouthed the words "I love you" before taking her usual seat by the bed, holding Mom's hand, thinking about her encounter with Dave Mackie and friends.

Thinking about Ajey Jadu. Trying to remember his father's name. Wondering if he was still a patient at the hospital. Om? Was that it? Sometimes she surprised herself with her memory. The trained police officer at the top of her game...

Well, perhaps no longer quite at the top . . .

After an hour or so she left her mother and wandered to the nursing station. The tiny Filipino nurse Jean had spoken to earlier looked up inquiringly from her computer screen. The name tag pinned to her breast read "Araw." Jean explained that she had run into an old friend and wondered if the friend's father was still in hospital. Jean thought she might visit. Om Jadu?

Araw's fingers flew over the keyboard for a moment before she declared that Om Jadu remained a patient. He was in Room 207.

The hospital was quiet at this time of the day. Patients lay in their beds, staring into space or watching TV screens bolted to the wall. The occasional visitor sat silently, attentively, at a patient's bedside. Occasionally, a nurse swished past. A couple of doctors inspected charts at a nursing station. Jean reached Room 207 just as Ajey Jadu came out. They nearly bumped into one another. He looked surprised.

"Well, hello," he said.

"Sorry, I was—" Jean, flustered.

"I was wondering how you and your mother are doing," Ajey said.

"I was with my mother," Jean said, recovering. "I thought I'd drop around and see how your father was doing."

"That's very kind," Ajey said.

"Any change?"

"No I'm afraid not. What about your mom?"

"Much the same," Jean said.

"I was just going to get myself some coffee. Would you join me?"

Jean hesitated and for an instant it flashed through her mind that this was not a good idea. But then she decided that the lines had been so blurred between what was a good idea and what was bad that she could no longer tell the difference. So she said, "Sure, that would be fine."

They took the elevator down to the cafeteria. It was all but deserted at that time of the afternoon. Ajey insisted on paying for their coffees and they seated themselves in a corner. Ajey wanted to know how she was adjusting to being back in Milton. Jean said it was good, spending time with her mother and helping her brother at the funeral home.

"That's right," Ajey said. "A family of undertakers."

"Yes, my father's father, and his father before that. We've been around Milton forever."

"But you decided that business wasn't for you?"

"I'm licensed and I worked with my father and brother for a time," Jean said. "But I wanted something else."

"Police work."

"That's right."

"But not anymore," Ajey said.

"No," she said. "Not anymore."

In case he decided this was the opening that would allow him to start asking questions about what had happened, she hurriedly added, "So here I am back where I started, helping out with the family business I had no intention of being involved in."

"Ironic," he said.

"Yes, I suppose it is," she said. "Be careful when it comes to announcing what you don't want to do or where you don't want to be, because you're liable to end up doing the thing you didn't want to do in the place you swore you'd never be."

"But this isn't going to be for all time, is it?"

"Right now I'm not too sure of anything," Jean said. "I'm just concentrating on my mother, making sure she's comfortable and well taken care of." She shrugged. "Waiting for the end, I guess."

"Get through this time with your mom, and then you can start to figure out what you want to do."

"What about you? You're not from Milton, are you?"

Ajey grinned, showing off those remarkably white teeth "The last place in the world I expected to live, let me tell you. I'm second generation, born in Toronto. My parents came here from Mumbai. I was in law school at the University of Toronto when my sister started to date Del. Family didn't like that one bit, of course, Del being older and not Hindu."

"I can imagine," Jean said.

"But they adapted. What else could they do? I graduated, Del and Sharma married, and the next thing he offered me a job with his development company. So now I am in Milton. My sister and I moved our parents to town a year ago. Then Dad got sick. And here we are. My life in a nutshell."

"How did you know Del was at school with my mother?"

Ajey issued another toothy grin. He sat back in his chair and seemed to appraise Jean before he answered. "I guess Del saw the stuff on the news about you. He told me he knew your mom. I told him she was not well. He sends his best."

"That's kind," Jean said. "I'm not sure how well they knew one another. She was a couple of years behind him."

"Small world here in Milton."

Jean nodded. "One of the reasons I wanted out—find a place where everyone didn't know your business."

"Did you find that place?"

She thought about it for a moment and then smiled. "No, I don't think I did."

"But now you're back," Ajey said. The statement came with a toothy smile, but it didn't help.

Jean covered up her agitation by saying, "Which reminds me, my brother encountered someone the other day who said she knew you."

"Yeah?" Ajey's smile remained in place. "Who was that?"

"Mandy?"

Ajey's smile diminished a few watts.

"She came into the funeral home to make arrangements for a friend of hers."

"She works in the Caulder office, I believe. But I don't know her except to say hello. I wonder how my name would come up." Jean was impressed by how Ajey could retain that smile and talk at the same time.

"That's a good question," Jean said. "She came to the funeral home about Shawna Simpson, I believe."

Ajey said, "I see."

"Did you know her? Shawna, I mean?"

"This is the woman they found out at the escarpment?"

"That's right."

"Doesn't ring a bell," Ajey said.

"She and Mandy being friends," Jean said.

Ajey looked at his watch. "I'd better go. Del will be wondering what's happened to me."

"Del keeps you on a pretty short leash?"

Ajey's grin looked forced. "Del is Del."

"That's what you said."

"What?"

"When we met the other day. 'Del is Del.'"

"It bears repeating." Ajey was on his feet, holding out his hand. "Great to see you, Jean."

Jean took his hand. It was cool to the touch. "Thank you for the coffee," she said.

"We'll do it again," he said.

He did not sound very enthusiastic about the prospect.

Screams could be heard coming from her mother's room as Jean came along the corridor. She hurried into the ward and found Araw with a couple of male nurses restraining an agitated Ida. She was making noises, her mouth twisted, trying to form words.

Araw looked up with a stricken expression. "We can't get Ida to settle down," she said, breathlessly.

Ida continued to struggle and cry out as the nurses fought to tie retraining straps around her wrists. Now what she was yelling began to take on understandable form—or appeared to. "Cleveland," she cried. "No! Cleveland! Cleveland!"

"Mom, Mom," Jean said, reaching Ida's side, placing a hand gently on her shoulder. "Mom, it's okay. It's okay."

Ida was wild-eyed and fearful, her mouth opening and closing, as though trying to get out more words that refused to be anything but garbled. Jean took her mother in her arms. The elderly woman trembled against her, so much skin and bone moving beneath her thin, flowered shift.

Gradually, her mother's voice was reduced to a whisper and her thin body began to relax. The wildness left her eyes, replaced by her more typical thousand-yard stare. Jean lowered her to the bed. Ida closed her eyes. Jean looked at Araw.

"What happened?"

Araw shook her head. "I don't know. I was at the nursing station and I heard her cry out. At first I couldn't believe it. She's never done this before. You know, she's spoken some words and tossed around a bit. But never as agitated and violent as this."

"I thought I saw someone in her room," said a heavy-set black man, one of the nurses who had restrained Ida.

"When was this?" Jean asked.

"An hour ago." He spoke with a lilting Caribbean inflection. "Mrs. Duncan down the hall was having some trouble. I just saw him out of the corner of my eye as I passed."

"But it was a male?" Jean said.

"I think so," the nurse said. "I didn't really get a good look at this person."

Jean turned to Araw. "But there was no one when you entered her room."

Araw looked distressed. "No, no," she said. "And if anyone had gone into her room, this person would have had to have passed my station. And I certainly didn't see anyone."

The heavyset nurse looked as though he wanted to comment, but then just shrugged as if to say, 'Whatever.'

"Thank you all," Jean said. "I really appreciate you coming to help my mother. I don't know where we would be without your help and support."

Both nurses looked pleased as they mumbled thanks before departing.

17

In the evening, still shaken from seeing her mother so distressed, Jean returned to the house after picking up the mail.

A postcard displayed a sunny view of Martindale Gardens, a senior citizen's home a block away. She flipped it over. The card was addressed to Bryce. Someone had written in a shaky hand:

Sorry to hear about your mom. We were friends as kids. Think a lot about her. Hope she comes out ok.

Sincerely,

Earl Stone

She laid the card to one side and sat at the desk, opening the sheet of paper the hospital nurses had provided. She added the word "Cleveland" to the list.

GARLOCK

FARGO

RATTLESNAKE

NIGHT

MURDER

CLEVELAND

For the next few minutes she sat staring at the words, once again grappling with what they might mean. If they meant anything.

"There is no mystery."

Jean swung around to find Bryce standing there.

"You're going to drive yourself crazy with this stuff," Bryce said.

"Mom had a terrible afternoon. Yelling and screaming. The nurses had to restrain her."

"For God's sake she's in a coma," Bryce said.

"She wasn't this afternoon. I got to the room and held her until she settled down."

"Thanks for being there for her," Bryce said in that formal voice he fell into when speaking of his mother.

"This came in the mail." Jean handed him the postcard.

Bryce glanced at it. "Earl Stone. Never heard of him."

"I guess he went to school with Mom. He's at Martindale Gardens."

"Nice." Bryce threw the postcard down on the desk.

Jean said, "I had coffee with Ajey Jadu."

Bryce looked at her. "Again?"

The sound of the front door chimes stopped Jean from answering. "Who could that be?" Bryce said in an agitated voice.

He went into the front hall and opened the door. Detective Mickey Dann said, "Good evening, Bryce. Have I got you at a bad time?"

Mickey was with another detective, a tall, grizzled-looking man wearing a windbreaker and an open-collared shirt.

"We were just about to have dinner," Bryce said.

"This won't take long," Mickey said. "Do you mind if we step inside?"

Bryce moved away from the door to allow the two men into the hallway. Everyone was suddenly crammed together. Mickey said, "This is Detective Glen Petrusiak."

Petrusiak offered his hand, and Bryce took it. The detective had iron gray hair receding along a high forehead. He looked as though he had been around the block a couple of times. "How are you, Bryce?"

"Glen, this is Bryce's sister, Jean."

"Hey, Jean," Petrusiak said. The two shook hands. "I hear you're with the Mounties."

"Not anymore," Jean said.

"I was with the Toronto police for ten years," Petrusiak said in a friendly voice. "Got to be too much."

"So now you're on the Milton force," Jean said.

"Great bunch of people out here," Petrusiak said. "Made me feel right at home."

"We keep him busy," Mickey said. "Is there somewhere we can sit and talk?"

"Let's go into the living room," Bryce said. "Can I get you anything gentlemen?"

"No, we're fine, thanks," Mickey said. He turned to Jean. "Jean, it might be better if we talk to Bryce alone."

"Why would it be better?"

That stopped Mickey momentarily. It was not the answer he had been expecting. "Let's put it this way, I'd prefer it if we spoke to Bryce alone."

"Mickey, you might prefer it that way. But here's what Bryce and I prefer. We prefer that I be present when you speak to him."

"Hey, this is just an informational chat, nothing more," said Glen Petrusiak, putting on a professional smile.

"Then you won't mind if I sit in," Jean said.

"I'd be a lot more comfortable if Jean stayed with us," Bryce chimed in.

"Sure," Mickey said. "That's not a problem."

"Glad to hear it," Jean said.

They filed into the living room. Mickey perched on the edge of the sofa and produced a notebook. Glen Petrusiak sat next to him. Bryce folded himself into an easy chair facing the sofa. He crossed his legs and tried not to look nervous. Jean didn't think he was doing a very good job of it. She sat on a bench against the wall facing the three men, functioning as a sort of ad hoc referee, keeping an eye on the participants in the game about to unfold.

Mickey looked at Bryce and said, "Detective Petrusiak and I are in charge of the investigation into the death of Shawna Simpson. As I said earlier, this is an information visit. We're talking to a lot of people, trying to put things together."

"Right," Bryce said.

"When I say Shawna Simpson's name, Bryce, I presume you know who I'm talking about?"

"Yes, of course," Bryce said. "We have her body here at the funeral home."

"Did you know the deceased?" Mickey asked.

To his credit, Jean thought, Bryce barely hesitated before he answered. "Yes," he said.

"Why didn't you say something when you picked up the body on the escarpment?" Mickey said.

"I wasn't sure," Bryce said. "It was still dark and obviously the body was in bad shape."

"So when did you know?"

"I wasn't certain until the body was released yesterday."

"And yet you still didn't say anything."

"By that time you had identified Shawna," Bryce said smoothly. Not quite the truth, Jean thought, but not a lie, either.

Petrusiak looked up from his notebook in which he had been writing. He had hard green eyes, Jean noticed. "Tell us where you were before being called up to the escarpment."

"I was with Shawna," Bryce said.

The ensuing silence produced an uncomfortable tension. Mickey cleared his throat. "What does that mean?"

"It means we were together at her apartment," Bryce said.

"The night she died?"

"That's correct."

Mickey looked abruptly impatient. "Help me out here, Bryce. What time was this?"

"I left around one o'clock. She was in bed. She seemed fine."

"How long were the two of you together?"

"I got there about eight o'clock. So let's say four and a half hours."

"No indication she was in any trouble?"

"None," Bryce said with a shake of his head.

"What about depression? Had she seemed depressed lately?"

"Not as far as I could tell," Bryce said.

Petrusiak's head shot up from his notebook, as though something momentous had just occurred to him. "Did the two of you fight that night?"

"No." Bryce seemed offended by the notion.

"You didn't fight, ever?"

"There was nothing to fight about," Bryce said.

"No relationship difficulties," Mickey said. "Nothing like that?"

"It wasn't that kind of relationship," Bryce replied. "I didn't see her often, and I didn't see her for very long when I did see her. We both knew what we were there for. There were no arguments."

"And what did you know you were there for?" Petrusiak asked.

"Sex," Bryce said.

"And she was fine with that?"

"She seemed to be, yes."

"So there is no reason, as far as you are concerned, why Shawna would want to jump off a cliff up at Rattlesnake Point?"

"No."

"So when you realized the identity of this torn, broken body you had sitting in the basement of your funeral home, I imagine you must have been pretty upset."

Bryce didn't say anything for a few long beats. Then he nodded and said, "Yes, of course."

"Bryce," Mickey interjected, "it doesn't look to me as though you're all that upset."

"What am I supposed to do, Mickey? Throw myself on the floor, screaming in agony? I was shocked, okay? I have been trying to wrap my head around what's happened."

"What do you think happened, Bryce?"

"I don't know," Bryce said. "I have no idea."

The two detectives traded glances. Then Petrusiak shifted around and leaned forward, focusing on Bryce. His green eyes looked harder than ever. "Let me tell you something, Bryce. These answers you're giving us, they're crap. I've sat here for the past few minutes taking notes, and I'm thinking all this time, 'this guy is lying through his teeth.'"

Bryce looked shaken for a moment, and then flustered. "I'm not lying," he insisted.

"Come on, Mickey," Jean interjected. "Bryce has done his best to answer your questions. You heard him. He's as mystified as anyone about what's happened."

"No," Petrusiak said, keeping his eyes fixed on Bryce. "This is bullshit. A woman is dead. You were the last person to see her alive. You're treating this like you made a wrong turn or something."

"Like hell I am," Bryce yelled.

"This is a potential murder investigation, pal," Petrusiak shot back. The veins stood out in his neck. "Right now, you are our number one suspect. So if you know anything, anything at all that can help convince us you're not in some way responsible for what happened to this woman, you'd better cut the crap and tell us."

Bryce sat back and took a deep breath. "I've told you everything I know," he said in a voice straining to remain calm.

"Here's the other thing, Bryce," Petrusiak said. "You've got Shawna's body. That's pretty convenient, isn't it? Allows you to hide any possible incriminating evidence."

"That's ridiculous," Jean focused her angry gaze on Mickey. "You released the body. Presumably the coroner retrieved any evidence before that happened."

Neither detective said anything. Petrusiak continued to stare hard at Bryce. Mickey made a show of closing his notebook. "Okay, I think that's all for now." He got to his feet.

"What about the teenage girl who was up there?" Jean said.

The two detectives looked at her as if she had just landed from Mars. "What about her?" Mickey said.

"How is she?"

"She's doing okay," Mickey said.

"Have you identified her yet?"

Mickey issued an uneasy smile. "There you go investigating the case again, Jean."

"I'm not investigating anything," she said. "But I would think the girl would be able to help you with your investigation. She was there. Can't she shed some light on what happened?"

"That's if the kid is connected with Shawna's death," Mickey said. "And that's a big if."

"You mean that girl just happened to be wandering up on the escarpment in the middle of the night?"

Mickey turned his gaze back to Bryce. "The point is, if you go anywhere in the next while, let us know, will you Bryce?"

Bryce didn't say anything. "Okay," Mickey said. "Thanks for your time. We will be in touch."

After the two detectives departed, Bryce exhaled loudly. He looked at Jean. "How do you think that went?"

"I think you'd better get a lawyer," Jean said.

18

Bryce ordered pizza from the little place in the mall around the corner—chicken, red peppers, anchovies, the way they both liked it. Bryce had a beer with the pizza. Jean stuck with sparkling water. They talked into the night about what to do next.

Jean didn't say anything, but she agreed with Mickey Dann and his aggressive friend Glen Petrusiak. Her brother was not being completely honest about what he knew. If he wasn't lying about Shawna Simpson, he certainly gave that impression.

Out loud, Jean said, "You didn't get home at one o'clock the night you were with Shawna," Jean said.

"I told the police I left her at that time. I'm not saying that's when I got home."

"It was after two when I heard you come in," Jean said.

"After I left Shawna, I drove around for a while."

"Why did you do that?"

"I don't know, restless I suppose, not wanting to come straight home."

"Did anyone see you?"

"Now you're starting to sound like Mickey Dann," Bryce said.

"Did anyone?"

"There aren't a lot of people on the streets of Milton at that time of the morning."

"Look, it's one thing to lie to those cops," Jean said. "I don't agree with it, obviously, but maybe I can understand it. But if you lie to me, then I can't help you, and you're on your own."

"I'm not lying to you," Bryce said, insistently.

"Then you are telling me selective truths," Jean said.

"You can't know that."

"I know you," Jean shot back.

Bryce moved a pizza slice around on his plate, as though trying to decide whether or not to eat it. He pushed the plate to one side and sat back. His gaze met Jean's. "What do you think is going to happen?"

"I can't say for sure, but I don't think they would have shown up here if they weren't pretty certain at this point that Shawna was murdered."

"And after tonight?"

"I don't know, but just to be on the safe side, I would get hold of a lawyer."

"So you think I'm going to be arrested?"

"It's a possibility."

Bryce looked genuinely shocked. "But I didn't kill her."

"I hope you didn't. I hope I'm wrong. I hope it turns out she jumped to her death."

"Come on, Jean. I'm your brother for God's sake."

"Brothers kill people all the time," Jean said.

"This brother didn't kill anyone." He shook his head in despair. "I mean, it's so crazy to even have to talk like this."

"I hope this works out differently," she said. "But for now, this is the way we have to talk. And you have to be honest with me."

For a second, she thought she saw a spark in his eyes indicating he was about to say something. But then the spark was gone, and Bryce's face regained its familiar mask, the professional solemnity employed for bereaved relatives— and sisters with whom he had decided to dodge an honest conversation.

"There's nothing," he said. "There's nothing more to tell you."

"Do you have a lawyer you could call?"

"You're serious about this lawyer thing?"

"It's not me you have to worry about, it's the Halton police. You heard this guy Petrusiak. You're their number one suspect."

"Hank Berry handles legal affairs for the business, same as he always has."

"You need a criminal lawyer—a good one."

"I don't exactly keep a list of criminal lawyers lying around."

"Then get in touch with Hank, see if he can recommend someone."

"You really think I need someone like that?"

"You shouldn't talk to the police any more without a lawyer present," Jean said.

"Advice from an expert," Bryce said ruefully.

"Just being careful," Jean said.

"Listen, I appreciate your concern, I do," Bryce said. "But right now they aren't even sure if Shawna was murdered. Isn't it possible, Petrusiak was just trying to scare me?"

"Yes, it's possible—and you're right, they don't appear to know for certain what happened to Shawna. Given the condition of the body, I imagine they're having trouble ascertaining whether she jumped or was pushed. Or whether she might have been killed someplace else, and then the body was transported up to the escarpment and thrown off the cliff."

"So calling around asking about possible criminal defense lawyers, may not be a good idea," Bryce said. "This is still a small town, and I've got a business to run. I call a lawyer and it starts all sorts of talk—not good for business. I'd rather keep a lid on this for as long as I can."

"It's up to you," Jean said with a sigh. "But they will be back and next time it will be at police headquarters, and you shouldn't be there without a lawyer."

"That's okay," Bryce said. He forced a smile. "By that time you will have gotten to the bottom of what happened to Shawna and I will be in the clear."

"Bryce, seriously, there's not a whole lot I can do."

"Sure there is," Bryce said. "You're a better investigator than Mickey Dann or that other guy will ever be—and you're my sister. It's a dynamite combination."

"No, it isn't Bryce. You can't count on me."

"Yes, I can," Bryce said, adamantly. "Yes, I can."

———

Mickey Dann dropped Glen Petrusiak at his car in the Halton Police parking lot, and then drove south on Ontario Street North until he reached Main and turned right. He left his car in the lot behind Bryden's Pub and went inside. He was running late, but she was still there. Her dark hair was loose and falling to her shoulders. She was dressed in a white blouse and a short plaid skirt that set off the dark stockings and the high-heeled shoes.

"Sorry I'm late," he said, joining her. "I was tied up with a case."

"Keeping our community safe," she said. "How can a girl complain?"

"I don't know how safe I'm keeping it," Mickey said. He signaled the bartender. "Give me a Stoli on the rocks, will you?" He turned to her. "Can I refresh your drink?"

"Isn't that a nice way of putting it? Yes, you certainly can refresh my drink." She looked at the bartender and said, "Vodka and tonic, for me, please. And hold the fruit."

She finished what remained of her drink, and raked a hand through her hair, causing her hoop earrings to jangle. He felt the heat rise in him. Good grief, how long had it been since he'd been turned on like this? A long time, he surmised.

"You don't have to get home?" A teasing tone in her voice.

"No, I'm fine."

"Who have you got waiting for you? What? A wife? Girlfriend?"

He shrugged. "We've been living together for a couple of years. It's not working out so well."

"I'll bet you're difficult to live with."

He grinned awkwardly. "That could be it, all right."

Their drinks arrived. He said a small prayer of thanks, busying himself picking up the glass and taking a sip of the Stoli. He felt the sting of the liquor on his throat, followed a moment later by its warmth flooding through him. That was better. He took another swallow. Talking to her about relationships made him uneasy.

"What about you?" he said placing his drink on the bar.

"What about me?"

"What's your status?"

"There's no one waiting for me at home if that's what you mean."

"That doesn't tell me much," Mickey said.

"It tells you enough."

Mandy Dragan smiled and raised her glass.

Mickey said, "You're not married?"

"I was married. Not anymore."

"You didn't like being married?"

"I didn't like being married to the guy I married."

"Dragan. What is that? Russian?"

"No, no, not Russian. Ukrainian."

"A nice Ukrainian girl," Mickey said.

She smiled and said, "Not that nice."

"You work with Del, is that right?"

"Why I'm not that nice."

He laughed, taking another sip of the Stoli, waited for it to warm his insides before he placed the glass on the bar. "You said on the phone that you had something to tell me about Shawna Simpson."

"She was a very close friend of mine."

"Yes, that's what you said."

"Shawna told me everything, and with Shawna, you know, there was a whole lot to tell."

"What did she tell you about?"

"A lot about the men she was seeing."

"Give me some names."

"Okay, but I don't want to get into trouble. You understand that?"

"You're not going to get into trouble, Mandy. You're just providing information, that's all."

"About Shawna's men."

"You keep coming back to that."

"Because it is men who kill women."

"Yes," Mickey said.

"Del Caulder," Mandy said.

Mickey put his glass down on the bar before he said, "I'm aware that you work for Del."

She nodded. "I introduced him to Shawna. That may have been a mistake."

"How's that?"

"It made another man very jealous."

"Who was that?"

"Bryce Whitlock," she said

19

"When Ida and me were in high school, this was still pretty much a farming community," Earl Stone said. "It was a small town. Everyone knew everyone."

In the cool of the evening, the light fading, Jean sat with the old man on a park bench across the street from Martindale Gardens. The bench looked over Mill Pond. In the light thrown from the pathway surrounding the pond, maple trees showed flashes of color. There was an autumnal crispness in the evening air, a hint of the coming winter, enough so that Earl huddled in a windbreaker zipped up to his chin. But he had wanted to come over here. He did this every night after dinner, he said, crossing the street from Martindale to sit by the pond, contemplating the world.

"It was a nice time back in the eighties. I remember Ida and a group of us went into Toronto to see Bruce Springsteen. Another time, we saw Levon Helm at the El Mocambo. You know, the guy from the Band?"

"Sure," Jean said. "Mom loved their music."

"Yeah, in those days recording artists put out albums, and we actually went out and bought them, no downloading on the Internet. Good times. Not a care in the world."

Earl aimed a smile of remembrance across the pond. He had a nice smile, Jean thought. The smile dropped years off a creased and weathered face framed with thinning white hair.

"Did you and Mom date?"

"No, no, we were just friends. That's what they used to say in those days. We're 'just friends.' I would like to have been more than that, mind you. Your mom was a darling, and I was secretly crazy about her. But she decided we were 'just friends.' I think she was nuts about someone else."

"Do you remember who that was?"

"I'm not sure I ever knew his name. Someone older, I think. A university guy. I remember all the girls were jealous. Ida was dating *a university guy*. Everyone else was stuck with pimply high school geeks like me."

"Mom's been saying some pretty strange things in the last while," Jean said. "I think she's referring to something in her past, maybe something bad that happened. Do you have any idea what that might be?"

"I thought your mom was in a coma."

"She is. That's the crazy thing. Every so often, she regains consciousness. It's as though something's bothering her, something that she's trying to communicate but can't."

"I don't know what that would be," Earl said. "We did the stupid things teenagers do—beer, a little dope, although it wasn't around much then. Beer was about as bad as it got. It was all pretty innocent, looking back on it."

Jean pulled the sheet of paper out of her pocket and showed it to Earl. "Do any of these words mean anything to you?"

"Hold on a minute." He extracted a pair of glasses from his windbreaker and put them on. Then he took the paper from Jean and studied it. "Okay," he said, looking up from the paper after a moment. "Garlock could be Jane Garlock. She was in high school with us. And there was a guy named Kip Cleveland who was on the football team. But the rest of it doesn't mean much. I guess Rattlesnake could be Rattlesnake Point. We went up there a fair amount to drink beer, and we did it at night. But that was about the extent of it."

"How well did you know Jane Garlock and Kip Cleveland?"

"I didn't know Kip at all, except as one of the football players. But Jane was a bit of a hottie, like Ida, capturing the hearts and minds of us adoring, slobbering males."

"How about Jane? Did you date her?"

"Nope, not her, either. Now Jane wasn't anything like your mom. She was kind of stuck up and arrogant, the prom queen type. Not that we had prom queens. They'd gotten rid of that sort of thing by the time I was in high school. But if there had been a prom queen, Jane definitely would have been in the running."

"Any idea what happened to her?"

"Sure," Earl said. "She went on to marry the last guy in the world I ever thought was going to amount to anything."

"Who was that?"

"Who else?" Earl said. "Lorne Caulder."

"You mean Del, don't you? Del Caulder."

"I know that's what they call him now. But in high school he was Lorne the Loser," Earl said. "I believe Del was his middle name. No one called him Del until he started to get rich."

———————

Bryce was working late downstairs at the funeral home, getting caught up with his bookkeeping when he heard the front door upstairs open and close. He got up from his desk and went into the hallway where stairs led up to the main floor. "Hello," he called.

"Hey," a female voice called back.

Bryce went up the stairs. Mandy Dragan leaned against the wall. She had a bottle of wine in her hand. A crooked smile played on her lips. "I'm checking on Shawna," she said in a slightly slurred voice.

"It's a little late, isn't it?"

"You're here, aren't you?" The smile widened and she raised her arm to show him the bottle. "I brought some wine. So we could toast Shawna."

"I don't think we should do this tonight," Bryce said. "Why don't you come back tomorrow?"

Her face hardened. "Let's do it now."

He studied her leaning against the wall, a little drunk, alluring in that short skirt showing off long stocking-clad legs, dark hair falling around her shoulders. Easy, Bryce, he thought to himself. This is where you get into trouble.

"All right," he said. "One drink and then I've got to get some sleep. It's been a long day."

"Sure," she said. "Let's have that drink."

"Come on we'll go into the other room."

"No." She shook her head. "Where is Shawna?"

She pushed herself away from the wall and swayed past him. "Let's go downstairs," she said, and before he could stop her, she started down.

"This isn't a good idea," he said, lamely.

"Yes, it is," she called back. "I'm full of good ideas."

He followed her down the stairs and found her swaying in the middle of the corridor, unsure where to go next. "Let me see her," she said. "I want to see Shawna."

"Let's not do that," he said.

"I was talking to the police earlier tonight." There was a threatening tone in her voice. "Your name came up."

"Mandy, don't do this," he said.

"Let me see her, and I'll tell you what the police are saying."

"I know what they are saying," Bryce said. "They were around here earlier. They know about Shawna and me. You can't blackmail me."

"Blackmail you?" She issued a snort of laughter. "No one's blackmailing anyone. But there's something you should know. Something I didn't tell the police."

"What is it?"

"Let me see Shawna first."

He thought about it for a moment and then said, "Come with me," he said.

She trailed him into the back where the storage lockers were located. It was dark back here. The only light came from the hallway. He crossed the room. Behind him he could hear the click of her heels on the tile floor. Shawna was in one of the refrigerated units. He pulled the drawer open. The uncertain light reflected off the body bag containing her remains. Mandy put the wine bottle on one of the worktables and stepped over to the open drawer. Her face was slack and sober. "Open it," she said.

"Mandy, you don't want to do this."

"I want to see. Open it." Her breath came in short gasps.

He reached down into the drawer and yanked at the zipper and pulled it down, opening the bag, exposing the jumble of bone and flesh that had been Shawna Simpson.

"Jesus," Mandy gasped. "Oh, Jesus."

She fell against him and for a moment he thought she was going to faint. But then she squirmed against him, thrusting her body against his, her skirt riding high on her hips. She reached up, her arms around his neck, her mouth finding his. She gasped again.

Angrily, he pushed her away. "What are you doing?"

Her mouth looked swollen, her eyes glazed. She came at him, a predatory animal clawing his face. He fell back against the open drawer, braced himself and shoved her away. She screamed something he couldn't understand and then turned and ran from the room, her heels a staccato sound in the darkness.

He lunged after her.

20

Mickey Dann drove to the top of the hill where Del Caulder had built his sprawling dream house. The west walls were of reinforced glass, providing the best views of the escarpment and the surrounding countryside. Parking his car adjacent to the house, Mickey could see bits and pieces of Milton as the trees below the house divested themselves of their leaves. You could also see the housing developments spreading out around the town, creeping south and west like an invading army—Del Caulder's army conquering the land.

Del must love the view. From up here, Mickey thought, not for the first time, he could believe he ruled the world. That was all Del needed. As long as he had his patch of ground and could build houses on it, Del remained the king.

He went toward the house. As he approached, the front door opened and Ajey Jadu appeared. Mickey groaned inwardly. He did not want to deal with this guy today. The whiteness of Ajey's smile seemed to light the doorway. In a dark place, Mickey thought, he would want Ajey and that smile.

"Hey, Mickey," Ajey said. "Good to see you." The two men shook hands.

"You ever go home, Ajey? Or does Del provide you with a cot in the hallway outside his bedroom."

"Are you kidding? I sleep at the bottom of Del's bed," Ajey said, that toothsome white smile firmly in place. "Come on in. He's waiting for you."

They crossed a foyer the size of a ballroom, and then along a marbled hallway to double doors that appeared to open magically—the entrance to the Wizard's lair, Mickey thought. Or maybe the dragon's cave.

Del Caulder waited on the other side of the door, standing with his back to Mickey, fists on his hips, staring out at the escarpment in the hazy distance.

Ajey said, "Mickey's here, Del."

Del swung around, his red face already twisted in irritation. "What the hell, Ajey. You don't think I know Mickey's here? You think I can't see him walk through the door? Jeez-Louise."

Del, as big as all outdoors, carrying three hundred pounds around so that he looked as though he might burst out of his clothes at any moment and explode across the room, taking everyone with him. His outbursts were as outsized as he was, and they always gave the impression they were laced with expletives, except he never quite got to the expletives. A tough guy who couldn't bring himself to swear, Mickey thought.

"I'll give the two of you the room," Ajey said calmly, as if the boss's agitation came with the territory.

"Yeah, please? Would you mind?"

"I'm outside if you need me," Ajey said.

"And don't you damned well be listening at the keyhole," Del yelled.

"There are no keyholes, Del," Ajey said, delivering one more gleaming smile before seeming to evaporate.

"That guy," Del said, his eyes on the door. "I have to put up with him. Otherwise his sister will kill me."

"I hear you can't get along without him," Mickey said.

Del looked horrified. "Who told you that crap? Hey, I'm Del Caulder, okay? I don't need anyone, you understand? How do you think I got to the top of this hill?"

"Ajey, the asshole who's packing heat he shouldn't be packing. He drove you up here."

"Part of Ajey's job. He carries a gun. You never know, right?" Del's eyes had narrowed. "Who told you he is carrying?"

"I get paid to know things," Mickey said. "You might tell Ajey to be more careful. He's a little too proud of the fact he can shoot somebody."

"Yeah, sure, Mickey, I'll have a talk with him." Now it was time for Del to break out the big smile. "How have you been, anyway? Everything okay? You want something to drink? Let me get you something. What would you like?"

"I'm okay, thanks, Del."

Del threw up his hands, as if giving into the inevitability of Mickey not wanting a drink. He ambled over to one of the big leather sofas positioned throughout the room, and threw himself onto it with a huge sigh. "Tell me some good news, Mickey," Del said. "Make me a happy man."

"If I knew that's why you called me up here, I could have figured something out," Mickey said. "Right now the only thing I can think of, I got a birthday coming up in two weeks."

Del's florid face took on a sour expression. "Your birthday? You think I give a s-h-i-t about your g.d. birthday? Give me a break, you jerk. What I want to hear about, what I can't find on the local g.d. newscasts is any word that you've fixed this Shawna Simpson thing."

"That's right. I forgot, Del. I forgot I was supposed to fix it. Remind me again. How the hell am I supposed to do that?"

Now Del was yelling. "You're supposed to make it go away. You're supposed to confirm that stupid kid for whatever g.d. reason jumped off a cliff so we can put an end to all this and get on with business. That's what you're supposed to do!"

Calmly, Mickey said, "We got a couple of problems with that, Del."

"What's the problem? She jumped off a cliff. End of story. And you know what? She wasn't that great, if you want to know the truth. I should have dumped her ass long ago. But, oh no. Nice guy Del Caulder. Now I've got all this crap to deal with."

"Yeah, well, the trouble is, every time we poke at this, someone pops up and makes noises like she didn't jump, that maybe she was pushed."

"That's a bunch of b.s.," Del said.

"A couple of names keep getting themselves attached to these noises."

Del filled the ensuing silence with heavy breathing, as though this conversation had left him breathless. "Is it hot in here? It feels hot in here. Is the air conditioning on?"

"How would I know, Del?"

He heaved himself to his feet and lumbered toward one of the windows, as if it was cooler the closer he got to a view of the escarpment. "Jeez-Louise," he said. "What names are we talking about?"

"One of the names is Bryce Whitlock," Mickey said.

For once, Del looked genuinely taken aback. "What the hell would Bryce Whitlock, the g.d. guy who runs a funeral home, have to do with Shawna?"

"He was with her the night she died."

"With her? What do you mean, *with* her? What's that supposed to mean?"

"It probably means he was screwing her," Mickey said.

That brought Del barreling back across the room, his face redder than ever. "What the hell are you talking about? He wasn't screwing her. He couldn't have been screwing her."

"Because you were screwing her, Del?"

That stopped him in mid-stride. He appeared more out of breath than ever. "Who told you that?"

"I mentioned two names. Yours is the other name."

"This is nuts. Who would be saying these things about me?" Del blinked a couple of times. His face had gone slack. "What? You think I had something to do with her death?" There was an incredulous note in his voice.

"You weren't jealous of her?"

"Why the hell would I be jealous?"

"Maybe because you found out she was screwing Bryce Whitlock."

Del worked his jaw around as if chewing on this proposition. "What'd I do to deserve this crap?" he said, finally.

"Maybe got yourself involved in something you shouldn't have been involved in," Mickey said.

"This isn't what I pay you for, Mickey."

"You don't pay me, Del."

"Call it whatever you like. Help for an old friend. A payday loan. Whatever. I want you to stop this crap about anyone killing her."

"Like I said, there are problems."

"What kind of problems?"

"Like how did she get up on the escarpment in the first place? Her car should have been parked in the lot, but it wasn't. It was still at her place. Also, there's the girl we found wandering nearby. We still don't know who she is, or what, if any, her association with Shawna was. Now we got information there might have been a motive for someone killing her."

"So what does that mean? Does that mean I'm a suspect?"

"It means we're not calling this an accident or a suicide. Not yet, anyway."

"So you're thinking, murder?"

"Let's just say the investigation is ongoing."

"Jeez-Louise."

"Let me ask you this, Del. Where were you the night she died?"

"I don't know. Here, I guess."

"What about your wife?"

"What about her?"

"Can she vouch for you?"

"Jeez, I don't want Sharma involved." His face was darkening again, anger regaining its hold.

"You may not have any choice," Mickey said.

"Look, I want you to handle this, okay? Whatever it takes, I don't care, just keep me out of it."

"It would help if you weren't involved in the first place," Mickey said.

"I'm not involved, not in the way you think. If you need a bad guy in this get on Bryce Whitlock's ass." Del forced a smile. "Hell, I'm a happily married man."

"Of course you are," Mickey said.

"Go after Bryce Whitlock. If it's murder, then he could be your man."

21

The memorial service for Shawna Simpson was held in the main reception room of the Whitlock Family Funeral Home. Attendance was sparse, no more than fifteen mourners, Bryce noted from his place at the back of the room.

He watched as Dave Mackie, who never did much of anything to help with the arrangements other than issue threats, lumbered past. Dave looked uncomfortable in a badly-fitted blue suit. Detective Mickey Dann was turned out better in unexpected pin stripes. Jean was elegant in a black sheath. Bryce had forgotten how nicely she could clean up. There was no sign of his uncle, Mayor Jock Whitlock, Shawna's boss. Not that he thought Jock would actually show up.

But still…

Bryce noticed his hand trembling. He felt nauseous and tired. What the hell was wrong with him? Of course, he knew what was wrong. The thing was he had to pull himself together and put on his game face for this.

Jean came over and said in a quiet voice, "What happened to your face?"

"What about my face?"

"Those scratches," she said.

He paused before he said, "I must have scratched myself in my sleep."

"You scratch yourself in your sleep?"

"I guess I'm not sleeping very well these nights."

"Are we waiting for Mandy Dragan?"

Bryce nodded. "She was supposed to have been here by now."

"You tried her cell?"

"I tried the number I have for her a couple of times. There's no answer."

"What are you going to do?"

"I don't know if it's up to me to do anything," he said.

She gave him a look. "You knew her, Bryce."

"Not well enough to speak at her funeral." She gave him another look. "All right. Let's give her another five minutes."

Ten minutes later there was still no sign of Mandy. The mourners shifted impatiently on the folding chairs lined up in front of the casket. They were here to bury the dead. Let's get on with it.

Bryce took a deep breath and stepped to the podium, checked to ensure that the microphone was on and said, "Good afternoon, ladies and gentlemen. Thanks for being here. My name is Bryce Whitlock, and, like all of you, I was a friend of Shawna's, and like all of you, I am devastated by her death."

He paused and for a moment Jean thought he might bolt from the podium. But he gathered himself together and continued: "I only knew Shawna briefly. I wish I'd gotten to know her better. She was a warm, intelligent young woman, bubbling with life, planning for a future in real estate. What happened to her should not have happened. It's not fair. I've been racking my brain ever since she left us, going over our moments together, searching for any clue that might help to understand how we have arrived at the place we find ourselves today. I must tell you, I have no answers. Only an overwhelming sense…"

This time Jean was sure he was going to lose it. "…an overwhelming sense of sadness and loss." The last words were choked out. As he finished, Bryce looked as if he was holding onto the sides of the podium for dear life. Slowly, he released his hands, stood very still for a moment or so, and then walked away from the podium, swaying down the aisle and out the door.

An uneasy silence fell over the room. Dave Mackie, looking angry, got to his feet and trudged out. Other mourners traded glances and shrugs. With nothing else to do, they began to vacate their seats and straggle away. Mickey Dann came and sat beside Jean.

"What was that all about?"

"He's upset," was all Jean could think of to say.

"Just so you know, Jean."

"What?"

"If that was designed to make me think he's not a suspect in this case, it didn't work," Mickey said.

"Can't fool a clever detective like you, right Mickey?"

He gave Jean a hostile look and then rose and followed the others out of the room, leaving her alone.

———————

Jean found Bryce on the deck at the rear of the house. He sat on one of the Adirondack chairs, sipping a beer, staring at the lawn. "I've got to cut the grass," he said when she appeared.

"I guess I don't have to ask if you're all right," she said.

"I'm sorry. I had to get the hell out of there."

"Yes," she said. "I guess you did."

"Did Mandy Dragan ever show up?"

"No. It ended after you left."

"Not much of a sendoff for Shawna."

"You made a pretty good speech—such as it was."

He looked up at her. She said, "We should make sure Mandy is all right."

Bryce didn't say anything.

"Do you have an address for her?"

"I believe she's in Oakville," Bryce said.

"Let's drive there," Jean said.

"I don't think that's necessary," Bryce said.

"I think it is."

Bryce put the beer on the deck and rose from the chair.

———————

Mandy lived in a townhouse complex off Bronte Road. Nearby was a large sign that announced this was the latest development from Caulder International, more evidence, Jean thought, of Del's desire to transform Milton from a sleepy farm town into a large bedroom community feeding Toronto and environs.

Bryce parked the car across the street. As they went to the front door, Jean could hear a baby's cry coming from one of the adjacent townhouses, the blare of rap music, somebody calling out. Bryce knocked and almost immediately the door opened.

Mickey Dann said, "Well, well. Look who's here. Come on in."

He stepped back to allow Bryce and Jean to enter. "We were worried when Mandy didn't show up at the memorial service," Jean said. "I guess you had the same thought, Mickey."

Detective Glen Petrusiak stood in the small living room. The four of them seemed to overwhelm the tight space. Jean looked around, taking in the coffee table and the white sofa, an incongruous recliner in front of a sixty-inch television screen.

"She's not here," Petrusiak said to no one in particular.

Mickey addressed Bryce. "You check on everyone who doesn't show up for a funeral?"

"Mandy made the funeral arrangements for Shawna with me," Bryce said smoothly. "When she didn't appear for the service today, I got worried."

"Why would Mandy make the arrangements?"

"She said Shawna had no family and she was a friend and would be taking care of the arrangements."

"She could do that?"

"I had to ensure there were no family members and then Mandy had to sign a waiver, but yes, she could."

"When is the last time you talked to her?"

"We were on the phone the other night making final arrangements."

"The other night being…?"

"Well, I guess it was last night," Bryce amended. Not very convincingly, Jean thought.

Mickey waited a couple of beats before he said. "And she seemed all right?"

"Yes, she did. She certainly gave no indication she wouldn't be at the memorial today."

Mickey waited a couple of long beats before he said, "Let's hope she turns up."

"Yes," Bryce replied.

"If you hear from her, let us know, will you?" This from Petrusiak.

"Of course," Bryce said.

By the time, they returned to the car, Bryce was taking deep, gulping breaths of air.

"Hey," Jean said. "I'm worried about you."

"I'm okay," Bryce said. "I'm fine. Let's get out of here. Do you mind driving?"

"No," she said, and got behind the wheel.

On the way back to the funeral home, Bryce stared straight ahead without saying anything. Jean cast a couple of worried glances in his direction but otherwise stayed silent. The uncommunicative brother and sister.

"There's something I should tell you," Bryce said finally.

"Oh, God, Bryce. Don't tell me you were lying to those detectives back there."

"I didn't talk to Mandy on the phone."

"What do you mean?"

"She came to the funeral home last night."

Jean closed her eyes for a moment, but didn't say anything.

"She showed up at the door about eleven o'clock, while you were still out. She'd been drinking. She wanted to see Shawna's body."

"You didn't show it to her, did you?"

"I shouldn't have, but under the circumstances, the way she was acting, I thought that was the easiest thing to do. Show her the body, and then get her out of there as soon as possible."

"So what happened?"

"We went downstairs, and I got the body out. As soon as that happened, she came at me. I think she had some crazy idea about having sex right there. I shoved her away. That really pissed her off. The next thing she was screaming at me, and clawing my face."

"Which explains the scratch marks."

"She called me a bastard a couple of times and then stumbled out of there."

"That was all of it?"

"Don't you think that was enough?" Bryce said.

"You didn't try to stop her?" Jean said. "You weren't worried that she'd been drinking and might be driving?"

"I was just relieved that she was gone," Bryce said.

"Again, you should have told those police officers what you've just told me," Jean said.

"I was afraid of how it would look."

"How do you think it's going to look when it turns out you were once again lying to them?"

Bryce didn't say anything.

22

Sharma Caulder, elegant, an intoxicating swirl of Jo Malone floating around her finely sculpted head, drove her husband up on the mountain to the spot where he planned on building The Heights.

"We are wasting our time," Sharma said as she parked the Cadillac at the side of the road.

"It's a beautiful day, let's enjoy it while we can," Del said,

"I'm telling you, it will never happen. You have already destroyed too much green space, people say. You are raping the land."

"You've been listening to my critics again," Del said.

"It's hard not to," Sharma retorted. "They are very loud and insistent."

"I'm not raping the land; I'm building for the future." Del opened the passenger door and began the increasingly arduous process of easing himself out. "And thanks for all your support."

"I am only being realistic," Sharma said. "There are too many people around you who only tell you what you want to hear."

"I need more people like that," Del said.

"Let my brother tell you lies. Your wife tells you truths."

Del ginned. "I should have married Ajey."

By now he was out of the car, huffing and puffing. He watched his wife come around the car, taking note of the skin-tight white jeans that showed her off to perfection. She gave him a look, and he immediately knew what was coming next. "And another thing," Sharma started.

"Don't say the 'W' word," Del snapped.

"You mean 'weight?' Is that the 'W' word I cannot mention?"

"That's the one," Del said."

"I can keep quiet. I can watch you grow fatter and fatter and then die. No problem."

Del moved his jaw around but didn't say anything. It was a beautiful, clear day. A warm breeze blew tendrils of Sharma's otherwise immaculate hair around her clear, lovely face. He could strangle her at times. But not today. He turned to gaze out at the valley. From up here he could see for miles. The views from the houses on The Heights would be fantastic, nothing else like it around here, he thought to himself.

Sharma came and stood beside him and took his hand. "I don't want to be on your back all the time."

"Then don't be."

"I worry about you," she said.

"I'm okay," he said.

"This is too much," she continued. "Everyone is angry. No one likes what you want to do."

"I like it," Del said. "That's the thing. *Me.* I like it. Therefore it's gonna get done."

"You are an arrogant son of a bitch," Sharma said.

"Watch your language," he said to her.

"And there are the other things."

"What other things are you talking about?"

"You know what I mean."

"I believe you enjoyed it as much as me, maybe more."

"I am not going to argue with you, Del. I am just afraid that it is out of control, and you are not paying enough attention."

"I am paying attention, don't worry."

"You believe you are somehow omnipotent and that is not true."

"Omnipotent? I'm not even sure what that means."

"It means you are human. Flesh and blood. Capable of making mistakes."

"I am not making mistakes."

"I hope not—for both our sakes, I hope not."

"I came up here to get away from all this crap, not to hear more of it."

"You cannot get away from it merely by driving to the top of a mountain," Sharma said.

Sharma, the philosopher, Del thought. Well, maybe she was right. But he would worry about the shit raining down on him later. For now, he took a deep breath, inhaling the view, enjoying the feel of the sun on his face.

And then his cellphone buzzed and vibrated—the real world interrupting his reverie. Del sighed and swiped the phone. A muffled voice said, "You ought to check out the field behind Mill Pond."

"What?" Del said.

"You want your problems to go away? The field behind Mill Pond, adjacent to a railway viaduct."

"Who is this?"

The line went dead.

———————

Jean got to her mother shortly after noon. The duty nurse, Achala, reported that Ida had had a quiet night. There had been no further eruptions.

Jean had been sitting at Ida's bedside for the better part of an hour when Jock Whitlock appeared at the doorway. He carried a cut glass vase containing daisies. When Jean cocked an eyebrow at them, Jock shrugged and looked sheepish. "They used to be her favorite," he said.

"The good news is you brought a vase," Jean said. "Otherwise, I'm not sure what we would have done with them."

He came into the room, and plunked the vase on the side table beside Ida's bed.

"There's another chair," Jean said, pointing across the room.

He retrieved the chair and placed it beside Jean and perched on its edge, leaning forward as if waiting for Ida to say something. It would be a long wait, Jean mused.

"How's she doing?" Jock asked.

"You can see for yourself," Jean said. "This is how she is. This is how she's doing."

"No more strange words?"

"There was quite an outburst the other day, but since then, nothing. I thought you couldn't bring yourself to visit. That you wanted to remember her the way she was."

"Guilt, I suppose. I'm sure I'll feel less like a selfish bastard after this visit."

"Sitting here does have its healing qualities," Jean said.

"You're very patient, Jean. You're a good daughter."

"Am I, Jock? Or am I just a disgraced cop with nothing else to do?"

"Except maybe keep your brother out of trouble."

She gave him a long look before she said, "So maybe it isn't just guilt that brought you here."

"You know Mandy Dragan works in the mayor's office."

"I thought she worked for Del Caulder."

"She does. Del employs her, but she also does part-time work for the mayor's office."

"You mean Mandy Dragan works for you."

"I don't have that much to do with her, but she's in the office."

"How did that happen?"

"I'm not sure. We needed help. I suppose Del recommended her."

"Because Shawna Simpson also worked for Del."

"Yes," Jock said.

"And Shawna and Mandy are—or were—friends. Now Shawna is dead and Mandy has disappeared, and you're nervous about being associated with all this."

Jock made a show of reaching forward and adjusting Ida's bedcovers before he said, "I'm not nervous."

"Are you sure about that?"

He leaned back in his chair. "I just want to make sure you're all right, Jean. Bryce, too. Bryce in particular."

"What are you hearing, Jock?"

He twisted his body around so that for the first time since he entered the room, he was addressing her, not her mother. "I know he was seeing Shawna. He was probably the last person to see her alive."

"Like I told your friend, Mickey. The last person to see Shawna alive was the person who killed her."

"So you think someone killed her." Jock made the sentence a statement.

"I think that's what the police think."

"And that person wasn't Bryce?"

"You know it wasn't Bryce."

"I don't know anything, Jean. Neither do you."

"I know this: no matter how it turns out with Shawna, Bryce hasn't killed anyone."

"I hope you're right," Jock said. He looked at his watch. "I'd better get to the office. Do you need anything?"

"No, I'm fine."

He heaved himself to his feet, looking down at Ida. His face abruptly fell into sadness. "She was a beauty in her day. Everyone fell a little bit in love with Ida Whitlock."

"What about a boy named Kip Cleveland?"

Jock's head shot up. He turned to Jean fighting not to show anything. Not doing a very good job of it.

"He was at school with you. He played on the football team."

"Yes, that's right. Running back, as I remember. A pretty good player. But how did you come up with that name?"

"Mom," Jean said.

Jock's eyebrows rose up and down. His mouth produced a sour expression. "Ida said his name?"

"That's right."

"I'm surprised. All these years later."

"Did they date?"

"They might have. I don't remember. It was a long time ago."

"What about someone in university she might have been dating?"

Jock shrugged. "She started seeing your father after she graduated from high school. I don't know anything about anyone in university."

"Earl Stone says he remembers hearing about someone in university. All her girlfriends were envious."

"Earl? Is that character still around?"

"He's living at Martindale Gardens."

Jock gave her one of his cool, appraising looks, the look Jean had seen him use when measuring his opposition. "You're quite the little sleuth, aren't you?"

"What about Kip Cleveland. Any idea what happened to him?"

"Now that's kind of interesting," Jock said. "Kip was adopted by the Clevelands here in Milton. But when he was in his twenties, he somehow tracked down his birth mother who was living in Toronto, and ended up taking her last name, Chartwell. His middle name is Carter, so now he's Carter Chartwell."

Jean looked at him blankly.

"That's right," Jock said. "You've been caught up fighting crime out West and in Afghanistan. You probably don't know about these cultural things. As Carter Chartwell, Kip has left his humble Milton beginnings far behind to become Toronto's number one theater impresario. Any of the big shows that come to town, Carter's the guy behind them."

Jock checked his watch again. "Now I really am running late." He leaned forward and kissed Jean on the forehead.

"Thanks for coming over, Jock. I know it's difficult for you, but Mom would appreciate it."

"I wonder about that," Jock said. "But I'm glad I dropped by."

He headed for the door and then paused, and turned back to her. "There's this old thing about sleeping dogs," he said.

"Letting them lie," Jean said.

"The past is past. Your mom's making a slow exit. Maybe it's better to let her do it in peace."

"Except I don't think she is at peace, Jock, and I wonder why."

He looked at her but didn't say anything. He went out the door and into the hall.

23

It was after eight before it got dark enough.

Dave Mackie put on coveralls and a pair of rubber boots, found the hockey equipment bag that would do the job, and then pulled out the shopping cart he kept at the rear of the garage and lifted it into the back of his Dodge Ram.

After that, he rewarded himself with what remained of his coke stash, chased with two or three—maybe it was four—Jack Daniels shots. By the time he drove the truck over and parked at the side of the roadway adjacent to Mill Pond, he was feeling pretty damned good—good enough to get through this. He pulled the shopping cart out the back of the truck, threw in the hockey bag, and then pushed the cart across the roadway to the set of concrete stairs leading up to the pond.

It was pretty well lit on the path running alongside the creek draining into the pond. When he reached the concrete spillway that bisected the calmer waters of the pond from the rushing waters of the creek, he parked the cart to one side, pulled on plastic gloves and extracted a Maglite LED flashlight from the pocket of his coveralls. He shone the light across the spillway. The beam outlined a distant railway overpass.

He lifted the hockey equipment bag out of the cart, took a deep breath and crossed the spillway. A weed-choked field ran up to the overpass. He crossed it and then clambered up the embankment to the tracks where he paused to catch his breath. The coke was playing tricks with his head. Maybe he shouldn't have done so much before starting out. He was feeling weird. He took a couple of deep breaths and shone the flashlight around on the ground below the far side of the embankment.

He couldn't see anything.

Dave huffed and puffed down the embankment, shining the flashlight around, illuminating green garbage bags and the rusted remains of a lawn mower—the crap that people had discarded here.

He found the body near one of the garbage bags. The Maglite showed the body lying face down, naked, dark hair tumbling forward. He turned the flashlight off and stood staring at the corpse.

It was a clear, starry night with a three-quarter moon shining down, empowering him, he imagined, infusing him with the strength of a wolf. The coke was working now. Or maybe it really was the moonlight. Either way, he had to do this.

He took another deep breath and then set to work, opening up the equipment bag. Then he took the body by the ankles. The body was loose and malleable. Rigor mortis had come and gone. The body had become slightly bloated. He struggled for a few minutes squeezing the corpse into the hockey bag, not the easiest thing to do. When the job was finally done, he zipped the bag shut.

He did a lot of cursing, lugging the equipment bag up the embankment, across the railroad tracks and then down again. He managed to carry it across the spillway and get it into the waiting shopping cart.

Dave soon discovered that wheeling the shopping cart back to his truck was considerably more difficult with a dead body in it. There must be a better way to do this, Dave mused. But then again, how often did he have to move a body around?

There was more difficulty getting the shopping cart down the steps. He pretty much had to lift up the cart with the body in it. The metal spokes dug into his fingers, causing bleeding, and making Dave swear more.

By the time he got the equipment bag into the truck and then loaded in the shopping cart, it was nearing midnight. He felt a sense of relief. He thought he might reward himself and stop off at Dobbs's place, but then he thought better of it. Buying the same shit back from the guy he had originally sold it to, that was a dumb idea. No, he would get home and drink more Jack Daniels.

"Excuse me." A voice from behind him.

Dave turned to find a police officer getting out of his cruiser on the driver side. A second officer was opening the door on the passenger side. Where did these guys come from? The goddamn coke made him careless. He should have heard them driving up behind him. Now it was too late.

"Hey," Dave said, trying to stay loose and relaxed as the officer approached. The cop was a young guy with a round, clear face, bareheaded, thinning brown hair. He looked to Dave like a chipmunk.

"How are you tonight?" the officer said. He was shining a flashlight. Behind him, Dave could see the second officer, also young, more muscular; someone who worked out.

"I'm doing okay. What's up?"

"You got some ID you can show us?" asked the young cop.

Dave dug his wallet out of his back pocket and fished out his driver's license. The young cop shone a light on it, and then passed it back to his partner. The second cop glanced at it and then started away toward the cruiser.

"You mind me asking you about that shopping cart in your truck." The young cop was shining the light on Dave now. What the hell? Dave thought. The shopping cart?

Dave said, "What about it?"

"We saw you wheeling it along the path by the creek," the young cop said.

"So what?"

"Is it yours?"

"Yeah, it is."

Dave could see the second cop in the cruiser, probably running a computer check on his driver's license.

"Do you mind if I ask where you got it?"

"I don't know, I guess I found it."

"You found it?"

"Yeah."

"Because, Dave, we've had reports of stolen shopping carts lately. You know the local supermarkets are up in arms. They want us to do something about it."

Dave just looked at him.

"The other thing here, it's unusual to see someone with his own shopping cart at this time of night."

Now the second cop was out of the cruiser, walking back with his driver's license.

The young cop was saying something. Dave tried to refocus. "What?"

"I said, do you mind telling me what you're doing out here at this time of night with a shopping cart."

"I don't know," Dave said. "What difference does it make?"

"Why don't you tell me what you're doing?"

"Looking for stuff," Dave said.

"Looking for stuff?" the young cop repeated. "You weren't stealing that shopping cart, were you, Dave?"

The second cop came abreast of his partner. He did not hand the driver's license back. He said, "Dave, it looks like there's an outstanding warrant on you."

"That's crazy," Dave said. He was having trouble focusing. That coke. He never should have touched it. There was a rushing in his ears, making it difficult to hear what the second cop was saying. Something about unpaid child support. That bitch. What the hell was she doing going to the police? The rushing in his ears got louder.

Dave turned and started running.

24

Three white and gold spires dominated the penthouse foyer of the Chartwell Building, a gleaming architect's model of the elegant condominium towers Carter Chartwell, the former Kip Cleveland, envisioned for Toronto. The spires, if and when completed, would dominate the cityscape, Carter Chartwell's legacy, the monument to himself, said his critics, many of whom sat on Toronto City Council and did not want his dream to become a reality.

Jean, standing in the reception area with its breathtaking view of Union Station on Front Street, the waterfront and Lake Ontario beyond, could not help but be impressed. She was embarrassed to admit to herself that she did not know about any of this before she Googled Chartwell, expecting to read about a theater mogul who brought Broadway musicals to town, not a developer with silver and gold spires in his dreams.

"What do you think?" a voice from behind her said.

The slim bald-headed man looked not at all like a Kip Cleveland, Jean thought to herself. However, he could certainly pass for someone named Carter Chartwell.

Jean could only say, "It's something."

"Yes," Chartwell said. "Something. Let's hope that's exactly what it is."

"Trouble?"

"Trouble doesn't begin to cover it," he said ruefully. "Let's just say there are some people in this city's planning department who lack creative vision."

"You are a long way from Milton," Jean said.

"Not so far," Chartwell replied with another dry smile. "Forty-five minutes down the road, really. Not far at all." He held out his hand. "You're Ida's daughter."

She took his hand. "Thank you for seeing me."

"I've been reading about you in the papers, haven't I?"

"I don't know," Jean said. "Have you?"

This time the smile was fleeting; gone in flash. "How is Ida?"

"Not well, I'm afraid. Suffering from early—well, they're not quite certain if it's Alzheimer's or another form of dementia. But whatever it is, it isn't good."

"So I hear, and I'm so sorry, Jean." He held out his arm, indicating a pair of entrance doors. "Come on back. Let's get comfortable. Would you like coffee? Water?"

"I'm fine, thanks."

He opened one of the doors and ushered her into a long carpeted corridor. She followed him past open spaces featuring young, attractive men and women peering at laptop screens or fiddling with cellphones.

"I have so many fond memories of your mother," Chartwell was saying. "You know, when we were teenagers, she was one of the few kids who didn't laugh at my love of Broadway musicals, and who didn't think I was gay because I saved my money to go to Toronto to see Melina Mercouri in *Ilya, Darling*. It's now a forgotten musical, but I saw it at the O'Keefe Centre, and I loved the music, Melina, everything about it. Nobody else understood, but Ida did."

"Mom was always very non-judgmental when Bryce and I were growing up," Jean said. "She supported me when I decided to become a member of the Mounted Police. Everyone else thought I was crazy."

"That was your ambition? Even as a kid?"

"Yes, it was," Jean said. "My girlfriends wanted to be doctors and nurses. I wanted to be a cop."

Chartwell opened a door at the far end and they entered a vast office with a north-facing view of the city. Lushly upholstered sofas were arranged so that visitors could keep their eye on the city while they tried to convince Chartwell his money would be well-spent investing with them.

He indicated one of the sofas and said, "Sit down, Jean. Are you sure you won't have something?"

Jean shook her head. "I won't take up too much of your time, Mr. Chartwell."

He seated himself on the other side of a coffee table you could land a helicopter on. He leaned forward, crossing his legs, displaying suede Ugg slip-ons, the picture of casual elegance, focused intently on Jean.

"So tell me how I can help you."

"This is somewhat difficult to explain," Jean began, "but my mother is in a coma. Yet she keeps crying out every so often, saying things that don't make sense."

"Understandable, I suppose, considering her condition," Chartwell said.

"Yes, except she shouldn't be saying anything at all. I have this sense that she is trying to tell me something, something from her past."

Chartwell blinked twice and the eyes lost their intensity. He sat back on the sofa. "I thought this was going to be something different," he said.

"Oh?" Jean said.

"I thought you might have come here looking for support for your mother."

"No, no, she's fine—at least as far as money goes, if that's what you mean."

"Financially, that's the sort of thing where I might be of assistance," Chartwell said. "As far as her past is concerned, I'm not so certain I can be much help in that department."

"One of the words she keeps repeating is Cleveland," Jean said. Chartwell looked at her blankly.

"When she knew you, your name was Kip Cleveland," Jean added.

"Ah, I see. You think she's saying my name."

"It's a possibility," Jean said. "That's why I wanted to meet with you, see if you knew something."

"It was all so long ago," Chartwell said. "Another lifetime. Ida and I dated briefly in high school, I remember that. I remember being thrilled that she was interested in me, no matter how briefly."

"What happened?"

"You mean what happened that we didn't date any longer? What always happens in these instances, I suppose. Your mom was young, lovely. Every boy at school was crazy about her. She went off and dated someone else who caught her eye."

Jean withdrew the black and white photographs from her shoulder bag. "I found these in her apartment."

To her surprise, Chartwell hesitated before he leaned forward to accept the photographs. He spread them on the coffee table in front of him, taking his time, inspecting each of the five photos.

"You say you found these in Ida's apartment?"

"That's right," Jean said.

"She kept them all these years," he said, a note of wonderment in his voice.

"Do you know who this is?"

Chartwell looked up at her. "Supposing I said I did, what good do you think it would do?"

"I'm not sure it would do any good at all."

"Children poking into their parents' secrets," he said, gathering the photos together and piling them neatly on top of one another. "I'm not sure how useful that is."

"I don't know," Jean said. "All I know is that my mother seems to be trying to reach out, to tell me something."

"Or maybe she's not trying to tell you anything. Maybe this is something she wouldn't want you to know. Bits and pieces are getting out, thanks to the state she is in. But perhaps a healthy, aware Ida would not want her daughter knowing certain things—just as there are things I suppose in my past I'd prefer my children not to know."

"Are there?"

"Are there what?"

"Are there things in your past involving my mother that you wouldn't want your children to know?"

Chartwell allowed another dry smile. "Yes, I can see you were a member of law enforcement." He pointed at the photos on the coffee table. "His name is Patrick Hamer. Patrick. Not Pat. He insisted on being called Patrick. I do remember that."

"And my mother went out with him?"

"Your mother didn't go out with him," Chartwell said. "She ran off with him."

For a moment, Jean didn't think she had heard him right. "Ran off? You mean she left town with this person?"

"You find that so unbelievable?"

"I can't imagine my mother running away with anyone."

"This is what I'm trying to tell you, Jean. There are secrets your parents probably want kept that way. I'm not so sure your mother wants you to know about this if she's kept it from you until now."

"But the thing is, Mr. Chartwell, I don't believe she's trying to keep it from me. I think it's just the opposite."

Chartwell focused his gaze out the window for a few moments. He appeared to be gathering his thoughts. "I don't know all that much," he said, finally. "I know Patrick was attending Queen's University. I don't think he grew up in Milton, but I'm not sure about that. She met him, like I say, while we dated. The next thing I knew, she was telling me it was over—you know, a teenage thing. I wasn't sure what 'over' even meant in those days. Had we even begun, really? Who knows? I mean, we went out a few times, a couple of movies, a dance, not much more than that.

"Anyway, I heard that she had left town with this guy. A bit of a scandal at the time as I recall. Then, a month or two later, I saw her on Main Street. I was passing in my car. We waved at each other, it registered she was back in town, and that was the last I saw of her."

"You never tried to get in touch?"

"There was no reason. That time I saw her on Main Street, I happened to be home for the weekend, but by then I had left Milton." He allowed the ghost of a smile. "Let's say I never looked back after I got to Toronto. For me, life didn't begin in Milton. It began in Toronto."

Jean's gaze briefly swept the room. "Yes, I can see that."

"After I met my wife, she swept away memories of lost high school romances." He shrugged. "And obviously Ida moved on, as well. She met and married your father, and I assume that was a happy marriage?"

"I think it was, yes."

"So then hopefully, everyone ended up happily ever after."

"Did you know my father?"

"Ned? Sure. We all sort of knew one another back then. He was a year or so behind me. But the Whitlocks owned the local funeral home, so I guess he had a certain amount of notoriety."

"Any idea what happened to Patrick Hamer?"

"I think he died," Chartwell said. "Some sort of accident. Something. I can't remember any details. But I don't think he lasted long."

"Do you remember where he died?"

He thought for a moment and then said, "Don't hold me to this, but I think his death occurred in Milton."

"But you said he wasn't from Milton."

"As I say, that's my vague memory. But I could be wrong." Chartwell looked at his watch. "Look at the time. I'm afraid I'm going to have to let you go."

Chartwell rose to his feet with Jean. "I really appreciate your time, Mr. Chartwell," she said. "This is probably meaningless, but thanks for indulging an overly curious daughter."

"I've always had a soft spot for Ida," he said. "The one that got away, I suppose. It's so sad to hear what's happened to her. A reminder of the mortality of all of us, the unpleasant reality that we are closer to the end than we are to the beginning."

"Do you mind if I ask you one more question," Jean said.

"Go ahead," Chartwell said.

"Why did you change your name?"

"I suppose back then I thought Kip Cleveland didn't have much authority. But Carter Chartwell. Who could say no to Carter Chartwell?"

"No one, apparently."

He grinned. "I wish that were true, but that was my crazy thinking at the time."

"Nothing to do with escaping your past?"

He hesitated longer than she expected before he said, "There wasn't much of a past to escape. But maybe you're right. Maybe I wanted to start all over again in the big city. I can certainly recall wanting to change my name, but beyond that I don't remember much about my thinking at that age, other than the fact that, for me, getting out of Milton was a given."

She held out her hand to him. "Thank you again, Mr. Chartwell."

He took her hand into his two hands. His eyes filled with unexpected warmth. "My best wishes go with you and for your mom."

"That's very kind of you," Jean said.

"Good luck," he said.

————

After Jean left, Chartwell sat staring out the window at the view of Toronto, something he almost never did these days. When his assistant buzzed him, he told her to hold his calls for the time being. From his pocket he withdrew the smart phone he used for personal calls, and poked out a number.

"I just had an interesting visitor who has caused me some discomfort," he said when the person on the other end came on the line. "Jean Whitlock." He paused, listening. "She's poking around in her mother's past."

He paused again for the person on the other end of the line. "Ordinarily, I wouldn't worry about it," Chartwell continued. "But this is a former police officer nosing around. I would prefer not to be the focus of this kind of attention, certainly not right now."

He listened for a few more moments, and then said, "What I would like to know is what you propose to do about this. I need you to act and act quickly."

25

Mickey Dann studied Dave Mackie's battered and bruised face for a while before he said, "Dave, you are in trouble."

Dave sat very still in the hard-backed chair, facing Mickey across the metal table in one of the interrogation rooms at Halton Police headquarters. He gave Mickey a lazy, disinterested look. "Is that so?" he said.

"Yeah, Dave that's so," Mickey said. "We catch you with a woman's body in the back of your pickup truck, I don't know, to me that is the definition of shitload of trouble. Or have I got this all wrong?"

"I didn't kill her," Dave said.

"You didn't kill who?"

Dave took his time answering. "I didn't kill whoever was in the back of my truck."

"Who was it in your truck, Dave?"

"I'm not saying. All I'm saying, I didn't kill her."

"You don't know the name of the woman in the back of your truck—jammed in a hockey equipment bag?"

"I'm not saying."

"Can you say how she came to be in your truck?"

"I found her."

"You found her. Where did you find her?"

"Out by the railroad tracks."

"You were out by the railroad tracks at midnight, Dave. What were you doing there?"

"Going for a walk," Dave mumbled.

"What?" Mickey leaned forward and cocked his ear toward Dave, as if trying to hear him better.

"Walking. I was walking."

"Walking at midnight, pushing a shopping cart?"

"I found the shopping cart out there," Dave said.

"Let me get this straight, Dave. You found a dead body out by the train tracks at midnight, and then you found a shopping cart to put it in."

"Yeah, I found the body, and I didn't want to leave it out there, so I spotted this shopping cart, and put the body in the cart so I could take it back and report what I found to the police." Dave had grown surer of his story.

"Yet when the police stopped you, you ran away."

"They beat the shit out of me."

"They subdued a fleeing felon who had just dumped a dead body in the back of his pickup truck," Mickey amended.

"They beat me up," Dave repeated in a sullen voice.

"One of the officers is in hospital with a concussion, Dave."

"That was an accident. He slipped and fell and hit his head."

Mickey sat back and gave Dave a hard look. Dave slumped in his seat and refused to look anywhere except at the table surface.

"Look at me, Dave. I want you to look at me."

Dave slowly raised his eyes to meet Mickey's intense gaze. "So here's the thing, Dave. You've been screwing up since you were a teenager. You're running some sort of drug business and using that shit-can garage of yours as a front. You know that; I know that. You're a smalltime asshole, so stupid that it's almost boring to arrest you.

"But this is a horse of a different color, Dave. This is murder. It's the murder of Mandy Dragan. Don't tell me you don't know her, because I know you do."

"I don't know her," Dave said.

"Now do I think you killed Mandy? I don't know, Dave. You say you didn't, and okay, maybe I can buy that. You're an asshole and a bully but whether you're a killer or not, that remains to be seen. But I'll tell you what you are right now, and that's an accessory to murder. We can nail you for that, no problem. That way we can put you away for most of the rest of your life."

Dave turned his eyes away from Mickey. He took a deep breath.

"Someone sent you out there to pick up that body. Tell me who, co-operate with me, and you just might not spend the rest of your life wearing a red jump suit."

Dave slowly let his breath out. He raised his head so that his eyes once again met Mickey's. He said, "I want a lawyer."

What with traffic, it was nearing seven by the time Jean got back to Milton. She thought about stopping to see her mother, and then decided against it. They would be getting her ready for bed at this hour, and Jean would only disturb the routine.

Bryce was in the kitchen pouring himself a glass of beer when she came into the house. He said, "You want a beer?"

"Not for me, thanks," Jean said. "I didn't know you drank beer."

"Once in a while," Bryce said. "Where were you?"

"I went into the city."

"How about a drink? A glass of wine?"

"You don't want to know what I was doing there?"

He looked at her. "They found Mandy's body."

That was a jolt, and she showed it. "I'm sorry," she said after a moment. "Where did they find her?"

"They're not saying much of anything at the moment, other than the fact that they found a body, and it's tentatively been identified as Mandy Dragan."

"Have the police been here?"

He smirked at her. "What? They find a body and they come to me?"

"You know what I mean."

"Not so far," Bryce said. He leaned against the counter and took a long drink from his glass of beer. "Okay, what you were doing in Toronto?"

"Talking to Carter Chartwell."

Bryce gave her a confused look. "The guy who does those stage shows?"

Jean nodded. "When he went to high school here, he was known as Kip Cleveland. Jock went to school with him."

"And he saw you?"

"He used to date Mom in high school. It turns out she threw him over for another boy. Someone named Patrick Hamer. He's the person in those photos I found. They ran off together."

"You're kidding. Mom left town with a guy?"

"When she was a teenager, yes."

"I don't believe it."

"I didn't either—until now."

"Where did she go?"

"Chartwell didn't know, but she came back to town pretty soon, without this guy, and I guess she met Dad, and that was that."

"And Carter Chartwell told you all this?"

"I think he's carried a bit of a torch for her all these years."

Bryce finished the rest of his beer and then went to the fridge. "I don't know why you're doing this," he said.

Jean watched him withdraw another beer. He closed the door and looked at her. "Do you?"

"Chartwell wondered the same thing. I told him I thought Mom was trying to tell us something—something she wants us to know."

"What did he say to that?"

"He thought it might be just the opposite, things she wouldn't want us to know."

"That's a possibility, isn't it?" He snapped the cap on the beer and began to pour liquid into his glass.

"But what is it about Mom's past that she might want to keep secret?"

"I don't know, the fact that she had this moment of youthful indiscretion? Maybe that's it. You go poking around in people's lives you start to find things they don't want you to know about."

"Are you talking about Mom or yourself?"

"Maybe I'm talking about us all."

That hung in the air. Bryce took a long swallow from his glass. Jean said, "Are you hungry? I hadn't thought about dinner."

"There's some chicken in the fridge," Bryce said.

"Chicken and more chicken," Jean said. "What would we have done if they hadn't invented chicken?"

"We Whitlocks would starve," Bryce said, smiling.

"You could be right," Jean said.

Bryce's smile disappeared. "She doesn't want us to know."

Jean looked at him.

"I know Mom," Bryce said. "No matter what you think, she doesn't want us to know."

26

Ida enjoyed a quiet night, according to nurse Achala when Jean arrived the next morning. She was at peace, Achala said with satisfaction.

Jean caught the tone in her voice. "What do you think?"

Achala produced a shy little smile. "I have seen this many times. Lovely Ida, I believe she is going away from us. It is a gentle journey, but it is a journey, and it has begun."

"What do the doctors say?"

The smile tightened. "The doctors will not tell you what I tell you. But I have been around the dying for a long time—like the other nurses on this ward. We know."

"How long?"

"Not long," Achala said. "But as I said, she is at peace. The demons that inhabited her have gone away."

Jean sat beside the bed, holding her mother's soft, cool hand. She thought about her meeting with Carter Chartwell, tried to imagine the two of them, young, dating, going to a movie together. What? Kissing during the movie? *Necking?* Isn't that what kids used to do? Did she do that? She couldn't remember. By the time she was a teenager kissing at the movies had probably become passé. There were so many other places to do that sort of thing.

She tried to imagine her mother kissing some guy, groping inside a darkened movie theater. For the life of her, she could not summon the image.

"Am I interrupting?"

She turned to see Ajey Jadu in the doorway. He was dressed in a tan suit that looked as though it had been pressed a moment before he appeared. The suit went nicely with the dazzling white of his smile. "I was just going down for a coffee. Can I get you something? Or maybe we could have a coffee together."

"Sure, let's do that," she said, getting up from the chair. "I could use some coffee."

"How's your mom doing?"

"Not very good," she said following him into the corridor. "The nurses are sending up warning signals."

"About?"

"The only thing they warn you about around here."

"There is always reason for hope," he said.

"But the time comes to be realistic," Jean said. "I'm afraid that's where we are."

They went down the stairs together. "What about your dad. How's he?"

"Better, I would say. Coming around. I don't get a chance to spend as much time here as I'd like."

"Del keeps you busy?"

Ajey flashed another of his trademark grins. "We have a lot on the go these days."

They entered the cafeteria. She took a seat while he went to get coffee. Her cellphone vibrated and buzzed in her jacket pocket. She pulled it out. It was the mayor's office. She opened the phone and Grace said, "Jock wonders if you're available for lunch."

"Yes, I guess so. What time does he want to meet?"

"How's one o'clock?" Grace said. "The usual place. Jock says he'll bring the sandwiches."

"I'll see him at one, Grace," Jean said.

"He'll be delighted," Grace said.

"I'm sure he'll be jumping up and down with anticipation," Jean said dryly.

"Now, now," Grace admonished. "He really does look forward to these lunches."

"One it is," Jean said.

Ajey returned with the coffee. "Problems?"

"No, just my uncle wanting to have lunch."

"Lunch with the mayor of Milton. Nice. He's not the easiest guy to get hold of."

"If he wants something from you, it's amazing how accessible he is."

"I guess he doesn't want anything from me." Ajey seated himself across the table.

"Be patient," Jean said. "Jock eventually wants something from everyone. Then he becomes your best friend in the world. There's only one way to avoid him."

"What's that?"

"That's to want something from Jock."

"Then I'm in trouble," Ajey said.

"You want something from him?"

"Not me so much. Del."

"Ah, well, Del," Jean said. "Del knows better. Del knows the secret of dealing with Jock."

"What's that?"

"Never ask Jock for anything," Jean said. "That's the secret."

"Maybe that's why Del's got me on the payroll," Ajey said.

"So you can ask Jock for something?"

Ajey sipped his coffee and made a face. "This is awful."

"The coffee or the thought of dealing with Jock?"

"The coffee, of course." Ajey let loose another of his flashing smiles.

She sat back suddenly, looking at him in a new way, slightly bemused by the thought. He shook his head. "What?"

"It occurs to me why we're having coffee," she said.

"What occurs to you?"

"So maybe I can help you get to Jock."

Ajey laughed out loud before replying with a question: "Can you?"

"What if I said I could?"

"I would start to think that maybe that's a little too easy."

"You would be right," Jean said. "What's more, I don't think I would be much help."

"No?"

"My uncle likes me to listen to him. His history of listening to me is, to say the least, sketchy."

Ajey laughed again and put his coffee to one side. "I really do hate this coffee."

Jean looked at her watch. "I'd better be going."

"Off to see the uncle."

"And ignore my own advice."

"How's that?"

"I'm about to ask him for something."

27

Ordinarily, when he called these lunches, Jock was already in place on the park bench fronting the old city hall.

But not today.

Jean arrived to find the bench empty. She seated herself and waited. The day was warm but gray and overcast, promising rain. Across the lawn, a boy and girl ran around the cenotaph, watched closely by their mother. A woman came along walking a big shaggy dog of indeterminate origin. Then Jock appeared, looking resplendent in a pinstripe suit, a perfectly-executed Windsor knot pressed against the white collar of his otherwise dazzling blue dress shirt. You could vote for a guy who looked like that, Jean thought, even though the perfectly-tailored mayor, incongruously, carried a couple of brown paper bags.

"Are you early or am I late?" Jock said as he approached.

"You are late," Jean said.

"Having to listen to people who want me to do what I don't want to do." Jock dropped onto the bench with a grunt.

"I was just telling someone that's exactly the wrong way to deal with you."

"Who did you say that to?"

"I'd better not say," Jean said. "Then he wouldn't stand a chance with you."

Jock issued another grunt and busied himself opening one of the paper bags. He handed a sandwich to her and said, "What?"

"I'm going to ask you something, and I want you to answer me truthfully."

"I thought that was the wrong way to deal with me."

"Nonetheless, I want you to be honest with me."

"When have I ever been dishonest with you?"

She gave him a look. He frowned at the ham sandwich he held in his hands. "I told them mustard not mayonnaise. They've given me mayonnaise."

"Why didn't you tell me Mom ran away when she was a teenager?"

Jock continued to glower at his sandwich. "That's not being dishonest with you," he said. "That's deciding not to tell you something that's none of your business."

"So it's true."

He looked up so that his eyes locked on hers. "Yes. It's true. But I guess I'm tempted to follow that by saying, so what?"

"Aren't you going to ask me how I know?"

"I know how you know." While Jean looked at him in surprise, Jock took a bite out of his sandwich. "Not bad," he said. "Even without the mustard."

"Don't tell me Carter Chartwell called you."

"I still call him Kip," Jock said, after swallowing his mouthful of sandwich.

"I don't believe it," Jean said.

"You should have asked me. You didn't have to drive all the way into Toronto."

"I didn't know until he told me."

"Like I said, it's no big deal."

"Big enough that Chartwell called you as soon as I left his office."

"He's only worried that you may be making a mountain out of a mole hill. That, as he probably told you, he's afraid things will get unearthed that Ida never would have wanted anyone to know about."

"So tell me what happened, Jock."

"Nothing *happened*. It was a teenage thing. Ida got involved with this guy—what was his name?"

"Patrick Hamer?"

"Yeah, that's the guy. She met him and then broke up with Kip, whom everyone liked. This other guy, he wasn't local. He wasn't one of us, so we worried about her. The next thing, she disappeared. Her mom and dad were beside themselves, of course. She was like seventeen at the time, and she'd never done anything like this before."

"Did they call the police?"

Jock shook his head. "It never got that far. Ida came back. She said she was okay, but she didn't want to talk about it. Where she'd been, anything like that."

"How long had she been gone?"

"Not long. Four days, maybe a week."

"And what happened to Patrick Hamer?"

Jock swallowed another bite of his sandwich before answering. "A few weeks later, they found his body. They weren't sure whether it was an accident or suicide."

"But he was dead."

"That's right," Jock said.

"Where did they find him?"

"At the bottom of the escarpment. It looked like he had fallen or jumped off the cliff."

"But I thought he wasn't from around here."

"That's right," Jock said. "If I remember correctly, he was going to university in Kingston."

"What was he doing up on the escarpment?"

Jock shrugged. "It was so long ago, Jean. If I ever knew, I've long since forgotten."

"How did Mom react?"

"I suppose she was pretty upset at the time," Jock said. "But you know, you're young, you get past these things. She met your father, and that was that."

"Except you were crazy about her, too."

Jock smiled and for a moment, his eyes filled with the glitter of something far away and fondly remembered. "In those days," he said, "everyone was in love with your mother."

Later, she would remember that was the moment her cellphone sounded and everything changed. She almost didn't answer it, but something told her that was not a good idea.

It was the nurse, Achala. Ida had taken a turn for the worse.

The family of Agatha Fontaine, aged ninety-three, guessed that perhaps fifty people would attend her memorial service. However, less than fifteen occupied the rows of folding chairs set up before the podium and the blown up photo of Agatha in happier times, surrounded by the grandchildren who did not come to say a final goodbye.

Bryce, in his dove-gray morning suit, stood at the back, surveying the mourners as Agatha's daughter, a woman in her seventies and not in good health herself, remembered bucolic summers with their mom at the family cottage on Kennisis Lake in the Haliburton Highlands. He thought of all the food laid out for the luncheon following the service, much too much food. He was wondering what to do with the leftovers when his cellphone vibrated in his pocket. He looked at the readout, saw that it was Jean, and stepped into the hallway. "What is it?" he said into the phone.

"I'm on my way to Mom," Jean said. "Something's happened. I think you'd better come right away."

Bryce glanced back at the room with its scattering of mourners. "I'm in the middle of something here."

"Bryce." Jean's voice was tight.

"All right. I'm on my way."

He closed his phone, took a deep breath, and told himself not to be irritated, that Jean was probably overreacting. There had been a number of false alarms, and this was probably one more. Still, this was their mother. He put his cellphone away and went out of the hallway into the foyer and then out the door to the parking lot. He was surprised to see Mickey Dann getting out of a blue sedan. Two other police cruisers were pulling into the lot.

Bryce came to a stop as Mickey approached. His face was hard. There was another man with him. Bryce realized it was Mickey's partner, Glen Petrusiak.

Mickey said, "Bryce Whitlock."

The detective paused, as if waiting for Bryce to agree that he was who he was. Bryce was aware of the uniformed officers hovering, expecting—what? That he would make a run for it?

Bryce became aware that Mickey was talking. "You are under arrest for the murder of Mandy Dragan."

In the confusion of his mind, he expected Mickey to say he was under arrest for the murder of Shawna Simpson. The fact that it was Mandy left him opening and closing his mouth, unable to get words out. Mickey turned him around and yanked his hands behind his back. He was aware of the hard steel of handcuffs being attached to his wrists. How many movies and TV shows had featured suspects being handcuffed? He had seen it a thousand times, but now here he was handcuffed. He couldn't believe it. This had to be happening to someone else.

Then this other person, this someone else, was hustled toward a police cruiser, hemmed in by uniformed officers. The rear door of the cruiser opened and his head was pushed forward, propelling him into the backseat. Stale odors assaulted his nostrils, the metal smell of the wire mesh separating him from the two officers in the front. The sound of a car motor starting up.

Bryce wanted to tell them about his mother, that there was an emergency and he had to get to her.

But he could not find the words.

28

Jean had been around the dead all her life. Growing up as part of a family of funeral directors, she had no choice but to get to know death. And then there was Afghanistan, and violent death, not ever far removed from it.

But nothing quite prepares you for the death of your own mother, Jean thought. In death, Ida was a shell of herself, as though her spirit had lifted out of her, leaving a dry, wizened carapace. The real Ida had gone off somewhere. Heaven? Who could say? But wherever she had gone, Jean concluded, she was not here any longer.

Jean could not bring herself to cry. She had found Achala weeping and praying by her mother's bedside when she arrived, and spent time consoling the nurse. A bizarre circumstance, she supposed, yet it kept her busy for a few minutes, and spared her thinking too much about her mother's end. After all, Ida had not been present for some time now, so her leaving was sad yes, but at the same time, somehow anti-climactic.

She looked at her watch. Bryce should have been here by now. She did not want to say over the phone that Ida was dead—just as Achala had not wanted to deliver the news that way. Be gentle with death; talk about it face-to-face. The phone seemed indecently remote, too easy a way to come out with the bad news.

Still, she hoped Bryce hadn't taken her call to mean there was no urgency. But then again, there was no urgency, was there? Not any longer. Too late for goodbyes; time only for the mourning of the dead and for that there was all the time in the world.

She sat there for another hour. Still no sign of Bryce. Achala appeared, took one look at Ida gentle on her death bed and broke into more tears. When she recovered, she asked Jean if she would like a visit from the chaplain. Jean said, no, that was fine. When

Achala left, Jean again tried Bryce's cellphone and got his voice-mail. "Please call me as soon as you can," she said. She tried the funeral home—and got another voicemail.

She was not quite sure why she called Mickey Dann at police headquarters, but as soon as she did, he came on the line. "Jean, I probably shouldn't be talking to you right now," he said.

"I'm looking for my brother," she said.

Mickey hesitated before he said, "He's been arrested."

Jean said, "Arrested? Arrested for what?"

"He's going to be charged with the murder of Mandy Dragan."

"That's ridiculous," was all she could think to say.

"I don't know if he's done anything about a lawyer," Mickey said. "You should probably contact someone."

"Can I see him?"

"Not at the moment," Mickey said. "Sorry, Jean. I have to go." And he hung up.

Numbed, she sat staring at her dead mother, thinking it was just as well Ida was gone and didn't have to deal with the fact that her son had been arrested for murder.

————————

Bryce sat in a holding cell for a couple of hours before officers handcuffed his hands in front of him and brought him upstairs to a white-walled interrogation room. The room contained a metal table and three chairs. The officers seated him in one of the chairs.

He waited only a few minutes before Mickey Dann in shirt-sleeves entered carrying a file folder. Trailing him was Glen Petrusiak, also in shirtsleeves.

"Hey, Bryce," Mickey said in a friendly voice.

"Here, let's do something about those cuffs," Petrusiak said. He produced a key that he used to remove the handcuffs from Bryce's wrists. He sat back, relieved to be free of the restraints. Petrusiak joined Mickey across the table.

"Can we get you anything?" Mickey, still with the friendly voice. Somehow, it didn't sound right coming out of him, Bryce thought, forced, the sort of voice they taught you to use in Interrogation 101, just before they dropped the hammer.

"I'm not going to say anything," Bryce said. "Not until I've spoken to a lawyer."

Petrusiak leaned forward, as if to get a better view of the suspect. "That's your right, certainly, Bryce. But we thought we'd have a talk with you before things got too heated up, you know, give us a chance to hear your side of the story."

"Maybe get to the bottom of this," Mickey added.

"I didn't kill Mandy Dragan or anyone else," Bryce said. "I know it, and I think you know it as well."

"That's interesting," Mickey said. "How do we know you didn't kill Mandy? How do we know that, Bryce?"

"This is a wild goose chase," Bryce said.

"Okay, fine," Petrusiak said in a reasonable voice. "Then convince us we should believe you. Make us understand that we have the wrong suspect in front of us."

"Like I say, I'd like to talk to my lawyer."

"That's not exactly convincing us, Bryce," Mickey said.

When Bryce didn't respond, Petrusiak's face hardened. "This isn't a wild goose chase, Bryce. You're not sitting here because *maybe* you killed Mandy. We *know* you killed her. We've got the evidence to back it up."

"That's not true," Bryce interjected. "You don't have the evidence because I didn't do it." Bryce focused on Mickey. "You should be looking at Del Caulder. You're taping this interrogation, right, Mickey? So there's no hiding this. Mandy told me she was scared of Del. She knew he and Shawna had been sleeping together. She was afraid Del had something to do with Shawna's death. She wasn't sure, but she knew Shawna was afraid of him, and Shawna was dead. Now she thought Del might be coming after her. The next thing, she's dead, and who conveniently finds her body? Dave Mackie, the guy who does Del's dirty work for him. I'm not the killer. Del's the guy you should have in here."

Somewhat to Bryce's surprise, that outburst—an outburst he had sworn to himself he was going to hold in until he'd talked to a lawyer—had the effect of reducing both detectives to silence. Petrusiak said nothing, except he shot Mickey a quick glance.

Mickey responded by pushing back his chair and jumping to his feet, body tense, angled toward Bryce. "We *have you*, man," he said. "Mandy knew you had killed her friend Shawna Simpson. You had to shut her down."

"No, no Mickey. You got it all wrong. There was no need for me to shut her down, but Del? Del had to keep her quiet."

"Hey, that's enough," Petrusiak interjected. He was sitting up straight now, glaring at Mickey. "Let's all take a deep breath. Okay?"

Mickey appeared to understand he had said too much. "Get him out of here," he said to Petrusiak.

"You've got the wrong guy," Bryce said. "What's more, I think you know it."

Petrusiak didn't say anything.

29

It took some time, but Jean finally pulled herself together. Feeling more clear-headed, she gathered Ida's meagre possessions: a wedding ring that had been placed in a bedside table, a few pairs of underwear, toiletries, slacks and a blouse hanging in the closet beside a brown overcoat. She placed the items into the recyclable shopping bag she found on the floor of the closet. Once that was done, she went out to the nursing station and thanked the women on duty for their support and care of her mother these past few weeks. Led by Achala, they told Jean how much they liked Ida, and what a lovely woman she was, such a good patient, even as her condition deteriorated.

"I guess now we will never know," Achala said, using a tissue to dab away more tears.

"Know what?" Jean said.

"Her words. What they meant. When she left, she took her words with her."

Jean said, "Yes, I suppose she did," thinking of Bryce, thinking how meaningless everything else was right now.

She was leaving the hospital when her cellphone rang. It was Bryce. He sounded preternaturally calm. "I guess you've heard by now," he said.

"Yes. When I couldn't get hold of you, I phoned Mickey Dann."

"They finally let me make a phone call," he said.

"How are you?" Jean said.

"Other than the fact I've been fingerprinted, and my mouth swabbed, a mug shot taken, and I'm under arrest for murder, I'm fine."

"I'm at the hospital," Jean said.

Silence for a moment. And then Bryce said, "Mom?"

"I'm afraid so."

More silence. Jean added, "She just slipped away. It was very peaceful."

"Yes," he said.

"We've got to get you a lawyer," Jean said.

"Get hold of Hank Berry. He can recommend someone. I'm going to be arraigned tomorrow morning."

"I'll call Hank," Jean said. "In the meantime, you know enough not to say anything to them, don't you?"

"They've already grilled me."

"But you didn't say anything."

"I've been charged with Mandy Dragan's murder. However, they think I killed Shawna Simpson and then murdered Mandy to keep her quiet."

"That doesn't make sense," Jean said, knowing as soon as the words came out of her mouth that it did, at least to the police.

"I told them they had the wrong guy. I told them they should be investigating Del Caulder. Not me."

"Is that true?"

"Shawna had been screwing around with Del and some teenage girl, according to Mandy. When Shawna turned up dead on the escarpment, Mandy was frightened. She thought Del might be responsible, and would be coming after her next."

"Mandy told you this?"

"Yes. That's what she told me."

"What did the police say?"

"They don't like it."

"Bryce," she said, "I will make this right for you."

"What can I say, sis? I'm counting on you. Right now, you're all I've got."

––––––––––

Mickey was in the parking lot about to get into his car when he saw Glen Petrusiak coming toward him. He closed the driver's side door and turned toward him. Petrusiak said, "What the hell was that all about back there?"

"Do you believe that crap he was spouting?"

"I don't know, Mickey. Should I believe it?"

Mickey said, "He's lying. There's nothing to it."

"Nothing to it? Are you sure?"

Mickey's eyes narrowed. "Hey, what are you getting at, Glen?"

"Who says I'm getting at anything? It's just that there's a lot of talk about how tight you are with Del Caulder," Petrusiak said.

"I'm not tight with Del Caulder," Mickey said.

"Then how the hell does this talk get started?"

"Look, Del and my old man, they went to high school together. When I needed some help financially in college, Del was there. But he did that for a lot of kids around town, not just me. Since then I've been out to his place a couple of times, you know, providing security for big parties he's thrown, that sort of thing. No big deal. Lots of guys on the force have done work for him."

"Yeah, well lots of guys on the force aren't involved in this investigation." Petrusiak heaved a sigh. "Up to now, I've ignored the talk. It's none of my business. But this is different. This threatens our case against this guy."

"Like I said, Bryce is lying through his teeth. We've got the goods on him, Glen. He killed Shawna and he killed Mandy."

"Okay, but back there we got a preview of what his defense is going to be. What looked like a good murder case a couple of hours ago now promises to be a mess starring the biggest name in town, complete with sex, and a cop who may or may not be on the take."

"I'm not on the take." Mickey stuck his face inches from Petrusiak's. His eyes were black with suppressed rage.

Petrusiak took a couple of steps back, but otherwise seemed unperturbed. "Let's hope for both our sakes you're not," he said.

Mickey arranged one of his reassuring smiles, the sort of smile that had always got him through. He put a reassuring hand on Petrusiak's shoulder. "This will work out fine," he said. "I've been around this town all my life. I know these people. They are not gonna believe Bryce's crap. We have to stick together, that's all, stay the course. See it through, and we'll be fine."

Petrusiak gave him a long, dark look. "Yeah, well, we'll see."

Mickey took his hand away.

30

Shit. Shit. *Shit...*

As he drove, Mickey pounded the wheel in exasperation. For the first time in his career as a cop, he was scared because—also for the first time—he was coming to the realization that some of the things he had been up to could get him into real trouble.

Damn that Petrusiak anyway, he thought as he drove. He was too—what? Well, he wasn't from around here; he didn't understand how things got done in this town, how you grew up knowing everyone, and how everyone gave each other a helping hand. That's all he'd gotten from Del from time to time, he told himself. Nothing more than that. Except now it was possible that Del had blood on that helping hand and everything Del had done for him could come back to haunt him.

So the trick was to make certain that didn't happen. Take action, that was the key, Mickey concluded as he turned onto Mill Street. Don't sit there and allow events to overwhelm you. Be proactive. Learn from your mistakes.

That's what he was going to do all right. Before it was too late.

He parked in the drive beside the rundown Mill Street house. Cassie Dubois sat on the sagging, peeling front porch, sucking on a cigarette, long stringy hair pushed back behind her ears, a large, lumpen woman in jeans and a T-shirt.

Cassie gave Mickey a blurry look as he came up to the porch. He didn't like the look of her at all. He felt more cold fear prickling at his spine. "Is she inside?" Mickey demanded.

Now those dull eyes turned away from him. "Cassie," he said. "Answer me. Is she inside?"

The screen door behind her opened and Howard, Cassie's common law husband, stepped out. Lank hair fell to bony shoulders barely covered by a T-shirt once white but that repeated washings had turned sickly gray. Howard held a beer can in his hand. Howard said, "She's not here." Howard made it sound as though that was the most natural thing in the world.

"What do you mean, 'she's not here?'"

Howard's face was sullen, a mixture of belligerence and too many beers to get the day started. "She took off," he said.

"The girl was left in your care," Mickey said, the words sounding lame even as they came out of his mouth. "Your job was to make sure she didn't 'take off.'"

"When we got up yesterday, she was gone." Cassie flicked ashes onto the ground beside the porch. "Wasn't much we could do about it."

"And you weren't going to call me?" Mickey asked angrily.

"Thought she'd be back," Howard said. "But that ain't happened."

"She was a whore," Cassie said, dismissively, as if that ended that. "Russian whore."

"It was your job to look after her," Mickey said.

"Yeah, well, you look after her," Cassie said.

"Her name wasn't even Judy."

"And she weren't no fifteen, either," added Cassie. "Then there is that fake mute stuff."

Mickey said, "What the hell are you talking about?"

Howard said, "We heard her talking Russkie or what sounded like Russkie on the phone."

"Another thing she was lying through her pretty teeth about," Cassie said. "Show you how much of a whore she was, she even tried to come on to Howard."

"I resisted her," Howard insisted.

"You sure as hell didn't try very hard," Cassie said.

Mickey thought about the deepening mess he now found himself in.

Shit.

When Jean reached Hank Berry, he suggested a criminal lawyer named Edgar St. Jude. Everyone called him Doc. His offices were in Oakville, but he had also handled high profile criminal cases in Toronto. He was very expensive, but also very good. Hank and Doc St. Jude had gone to the University of Toronto law school together. He was called Doc because he had started out in medicine at McGill University in Montreal before switching to law at U of T. Hank agreed to give him a call.

Doc St. Jude telephoned late in the afternoon. He said he had already been in touch with the Halton crown prosecutor's office. Bryce was to be arraigned the next morning, charged with first degree murder.

"They think he *planned* Mandy Dragan's murder?" Jean didn't try to keep the surprise out of her voice.

"That appears to be what they are alleging," Doc said.

"Bryce didn't kill anyone, let alone plan it."

"Let's not worry about that right now," Doc said. "The charge is what it is. The first thing is to get him out of jail. Given the severity of the charge and the profile of the case, that's not going to be easy."

"The profile?" Jean said.

"From what Hank tells me, your family is prominent in the community. Long time funeral home owners, that sort of thing. Your uncle is the town mayor. And Jean, well, let's say your name has been in the papers recently."

"What's that got to do with anything?"

"Nothing, really," Doc replied, "except that everyone, including the media, is going to be paying a lot of attention, which means the crown is probably going to play hardball."

"Yes, I guess that makes sense," Jean said.

"But your brother's a longtime resident of the community—"

"He's lived here all his life," Jean interjected.

"He has no criminal record, I take it."

"No, of course not," Jean said.

"It's going to be expensive," Doc said. "Are you prepared for that?"

"Whatever it takes," Jean said.

"Then I'll see you tomorrow morning," Doc said.

She hung up the phone and sat very still for a time, her mind swirling with thoughts of her mother dead and Bryce in jail. Irrationally, it struck her that they were all going to die, that this was finite: her troubles with the Mounties, her brother, this world, this life surrounded by death. Soon enough she would join the dead. They all would, and everything they struggled through would be pointless. Everything would end. There would be no victories, no exoneration, no innocence or guilt.

Only the dead.

She began to weep then. She did not do this. She never cried. But here she was, crying. She bent forward, holding her face in her hands, her whole body shaking, the tears pouring down her face through her fingers.

31

Jean met Doc St. Jude inside the Halton County Courthouse at nine-thirty the next morning. Sandy-haired, pudgy-faced, in his mid-fifties, Doc walked with a pronounced limp. "I had polio as a child," he explained after they shook hands. "I always tell my clients that right off the top. I also tell them that polio has taught me never to stop, never to give up. This seems to provide them with reassurance."

"Well, then, I am reassured," Jean said with a smile.

They sat together on a bench outside the courtroom.

"I spoke to your brother this morning, just to introduce myself," Doc said. "I'm not telling you anything you don't already know. This is a preliminary hearing in front of a justice of the peace to establish a date for a bail hearing. It will be over in a couple of minutes."

"Do you think you can get him bail?"

"You know that we only get one kick at the can here, and this is a murder charge. Serious stuff, obviously. You're a former police officer. You've seen a fair number of cases before the courts, I would guess. Would you grant Bryce bail?"

"He's not a flight risk, so yes, I would," Jean replied. "But then I'm somewhat prejudiced, aren't I?"

"Let's be honest, it's rare for someone in your brother's position to get out on a bond. And like I said on the phone, it's going to be expensive."

"Whatever is necessary," Jean said.

"And you would act as his surety, I assume?"

"Yes, of course."

"Very well then," Doc said, slapping his knees with both hands and pushing himself up off the bench. "Let's go in there and see what we can do."

Courtroom number eight was done in blond wood like a suburban Swedish rec room. Pew-like seats faced the magistrate's bench. Presently, a door opened and prisoners filed in, twelve of them. Bryce was sixth in line. He was unshaven and looked tired. When he saw Jean, he gave a wan smile. The prisoners were seated to the right of the bench. Then the justice of the peace appeared, a small, red-faced man who gave Jean the impression he had stayed up too late on too many nights.

Once the justice was seated and had said good morning to the court, an assistant crown attorney, a young woman in a black robe, read the first degree murder charge against Bryce. Doc St. Jude stood and asked the justice of the peace to put over the case for three days. With no objections from the Crown, the justice named a date in three days.

And that was that. Jean followed Doc. St. Jude as he limped out of the court. He moved with his whole body bent forward, as if in a strong wind, determined to plough forward, no matter what.

Outside, she said to him, "Where do we go from here?"

"Now the Crown has to provide us with information as to what kind of case they have. That should come in the next day or so, although sometimes they dick around and try to delay. We'll see how they treat this. Then I'll sit down with Bryce, hear what he has to say, and put together an argument for his bail. Usually it's the Crown trying to demonstrate to a magistrate why an accused shouldn't be let out of jail. But in a case like this, involving a murder charge, it switches, and it's up to the defense to demonstrate that the Crown's case is weak enough, the accused is pure enough, and dependable enough to be set free until trial."

"Is there anything I can do to help?"

"Sure there is," Doc promptly replied. "In fact you are in a unique position to help your brother."

"Am I?"

"You are a former police officer, skilled in investigative techniques. If you believe your brother innocent then get to work, find out who is guilty—get the person who murdered Mandy Dragan."

———————

Jean came out of the courthouse, taking deep breaths. She had been in dozens of courtrooms, sat through any number of similar hearings, unmoved. But this time was different. This time it was her brother in the prisoner box. It was surreal. And now she was supposed to prove his innocence. There was a danger in that, of course. Supposing she found the killer, and it was Bryce?

What was she supposed to do then?

"Are you okay, Jean?"

She turned to see Mickey Dann standing a few feet away, smoking a cigarette.

Jean said, "I didn't know you smoked."

"I don't," Mickey said. He delivered a smile, and then dropped the cigarette to the step and ground it out with the heel of his shoe. He bent down, picked up the butt and transported it over to a nearby waste basket and dropped it in.

"I'm sorry about all this," Mickey said.

"I can't tell you how many times I said that when I was in your position—and didn't mean it," Jean said.

"Hey, I went to high school with you and Bryce. This isn't easy."

"He's innocent," Jean said.

"You know I can't discuss the case. I shouldn't even be talking to you."

"Then don't."

Mickey looked as if he was about to say something, then thought better of it. "Take care, Jean," he said.

"Don't smoke, Mickey," she said. "It's bad for you."

He flashed another smile. "Thanks for the advice."

She watched him walk back toward the courthouse.

32

By the time Jean returned to the funeral home, Ida's body lay in one of the viewing rooms, covered by a sheet so that only her head was visible. Doris Stamper had combed Ida's hair and arranged her facial features so that she looked less like someone reacting in shock as her soul tore out of her body. Today, Ida appeared to be at peace.

Jean sat with Ida for a long time, the way she had sat with her over these last weeks. She felt better here with her mom. Even in death, Ida could calm her daughter, make it possible for her to think through things. That had always been her mother's strength, the calmness in the face of whatever crisis her daughter encountered. Jean was just as glad her mom never knew about what had happened to Bryce.

But if she had known, what would she have advised?

Go back to the beginning, Jean, Ida might have said, back to the escarpment. Either Shawna had jumped, or someone pushed her off the cliff. Whatever happened up there led to the death of Mandy Dragan. Two dead women; the journey to their deaths had begun on the escarpment. Had the police found everything that could be found at the murder scene? These were local cops, after all.

Maybe they had missed something.

———

In the afternoon, Jean drove Bryce's truck up Steeles Avenue toward the escarpment. The sky was overcast as she reached the top of the hill and went along the roadway to Rattlesnake Point. She paid the attendant the entrance fee and then followed the road to the parking area.

In her high school English classes, she would have written about the forest dressed in bright autumn colors, and that was true today. She got out of the truck, inhaling the cool, fresh air. Yes, this was better, she thought. Up here, she could see things more clearly. See what, though? That her brother was a killer who murdered at least one woman and maybe two? If she was still a cop, and Bryce wasn't her brother, that's how she would be thinking right now.

But she was no longer a cop, and Bryce *was* her brother—and she could not think in such negative terms. She must believe he was innocent. That way she could help him. She was no use to Bryce thinking like a cop, thinking he, like everyone else in a cop's world, was guilty.

She followed the path through trees, per old high school essays, bright with a coat of autumnal colors. She thought more people would be up here at this time of year, but on a gloomy weekday afternoon, she found herself alone.

Reaching the staircase near the cliff edge where Shawna Simpson had met her end, Jean came to a stop. The area was pretty much as she remembered from that morning. The stairs descended to a wide landing, and then continued to the ground below. Bolts hammered into the rock by climbers remained in place to mark their passing. Blue and yellow nylon climbing ropes tied off around tree trunks disappeared over the cliff.

Beyond the cliff, the Lowville Valley showed itself in vibrant fall colors, neatly laid out fields, spreading to distant Lake Ontario and Mount Nemo. Derry Road was stitched in a straight line across the valley's floor. Adjacent to the roadway, she realized with a start, was Mayor Jock's spanking new house. No, house didn't properly describe what she was looking at from this high vantage point. More like Jock's Xanadu. What was he doing with such a place? she wondered. What the hell would he do with all that space? Who would clean it? Well, she supposed, if you could afford that house, then you could afford someone to clean it.

Except, how did Jock afford the house?

She made her way down the stairs and stood on the landing, studying the rock face where the cliff had split off to form a rock chimney. Shawna had tumbled down between the chimney and the cliff, ending up on the ground below the staircase, not all the way to the bottom, but far enough so that the force of the landing tore her body apart. Whether or not she was dead as she went off the cliff—well, that was the question, wasn't it?

Jean heard a sound from above and looked up to see the face of a girl peering down at her. Jean realized with a start of recognition that it was the same kid she encountered the morning they recovered Shawna's body; the mystery teenager who supposedly had been taken in hand by child welfare.

"Hey!" she called up.

The face promptly disappeared.

She hurried up the stairs. At the top, there was no sign of the girl, but Jean heard someone moving through the trees to the north. She started after the sound.

Ahead, she could see a figure dart away, scrambling up a rock-strewn hill. She called again. The figure, all but lost among masses of turning leaves, came to a stop as Jean, out of breath, reached her.

She said in a heavily-accented voice, "I need help."

33

They sat on a bench, not far from the staircase. Seeing her again in daylight, up close, the girl looked older than Jean remembered. She said her name was Tanya. She said she was fourteen years old. She spoke with what sounded like a Russian accent. No, Ukrainian, Tanya said. From Odessa.

"I thought the police took you to a foster home," Jean said.

The girl shook her head. "The home of Howard and Cassie. But I didn't like it there. They drink. Lots of drugs. One night, Howard came into my room, very drunk. He wanted to sleep with me, but I did not want to sleep with him. So I ran away."

"You've been living up here?"

"Not living. Existing. Like an animal."

"But why? Why didn't you go to the police?"

She looked down and didn't say anything.

"You can't tell me why?" Jean said.

"I prefer not," Tanya said.

"Are you afraid?"

Tanya studied small hands nestled in her lap.

"Tanya, I can help, but there's not much I can do if I don't know what it is you're afraid of."

"What is it that any woman is afraid of?"

Jean looked at her. "Men?"

Tanya shrugged. "The only thing."

The wisdom of a Ukrainian teenager, Jean thought.

Out loud she said, "I can protect you from this Howard."

"It is not only him."

"Then who?"

Silence.

"You can't stay up here," Jean said.

"Yes, this I know."

Jean thought about it a moment, and then said, "Come with me."

"You will turn me over to the police," Tanya said in an accusing voice.

"Not if you don't want me to."

"I'm not sure you can protect me from them," Tanya said.

"Who? Who do you need protection from? Where were you before you came up here?"

Tanya rose from the bench and started toward the cliff. Jean got up and followed her. "Tanya?"

She lifted her arm and reached out a finger. "There," she said.

Jean followed the line of her finger. "Down there? Where?"

"That house," Tanya said. "That's where I was."

Mayor Jock Whitlock's dream house.

Shaken, Jean swallowed and then said, "You stayed there?"

"A beautiful house," Tanya said.

"But you said you lived with this Howard and Cassie."

"Later I was with them."

"What happened in that house?" Jean asked. "Why didn't you want to stay?"

Tanya turned and gave Jean an appraising look, a more mature gaze than Jean would have imagined for someone so young. "Why do you do this?"

"Do what?"

"Why do you help me? What is in it for you?"

"Does there have to be anything?"

Her smile took on a cynical edge. "There is always something. Kindness is the lie you tell until you get what you want. My father used to say that."

"You're a young girl, all alone out here, and in trouble, come on, what would you expect me to do?"

Tanya just looked at her and didn't answer. Jean added, "And I know more about men and fear than you imagine."

Tanya turned away from the spreading view below. "Maybe I will come with you," she said. "Maybe you will be nicer."

"I've got a truck in the parking lot," Jean said.

"I have some things I must pick up," Tanya said.

"Okay," Jean said. "I'll follow you."

They went off the path, through a thicket of tall oak and maple trees, up a slope carpeted with leaves to a small clearing. Here Tanya had gathered fallen tree branches and formed them into a tepee-shaped lean-to braced around a tree trunk. A backpack lay on the floor of the lean-to. Tanya bent down and picked it up. When she straightened she said, "You should not trust so easily."

"What?" Jean said.

A blurred figure emerged from nearby maple trees. An arm was raised and then the crashing blow, the numbing pain, and literally, stars exploding through the trees and the leaves, driving away the yellows and reds and oranges of autumn. Jean was aware of falling, hearing Tanya in the background saying something.

Just before everything crashed into darkness.

34

Mayor Jock Whitlock peered out through the floor-to-ceiling windows at the faint outlines of the Toronto skyline all but lost in the late afternoon gloom.

"I look out here every day," said Del Caulder coming to stand beside Jock. "And every day I remind myself of my vision."

"And what's that, Del?"

"To build a single shining community from here to Toronto, a place for everyone to live."

"Yeah? What about farmers? How are you going to feed everyone if you pave over all the farmland?"

Del waved a disdainful hand. "Farmers, come on, Jock. You're talking old school. Listen, there are lots of people who want to feed us. We got too much g.d. food, you ask me. But what happens when people don't have a *place* where they can eat? Think about that. No, we gotta grow, expand."

Del put his arm around Jock's shoulder. "And that's where you come in, Jock. You're helping to fulfill that vision, to make possible the growth we all need."

"Isn't that the speech you gave to the Kiwanis a couple of months ago?"

Del took his arm away from Jock's shoulder. "That's the trouble with you. You actually listen to these g.d. speeches."

"Am I helping you fulfill your vision, Del? Or just helping you run for cover?"

Before Del had to answer, Mickey Dann's reflection appeared in the window. "Sounds like I've interrupted a philosophical discussion," Mickey said dryly.

Del moved away from the window, flashing a smile. "Just a couple of old friends shooting the breeze, waiting for you to show up."

Mickey eyed Jock uneasily before he said, "The mayor will be glad to know, I was out earning my paycheck from the municipality."

Del looked impatiently at his watch. "Where the hell is Ajey? He was supposed to be here."

"Out doing your bidding, Del," Mickey said sarcastically.

"If he was doing my g.d. bidding, as you call it, he'd be here by now. You want something to drink?"

Mickey shook his head. "I'm fine, Del. What's this about, anyway? Why are we here?"

"We are here," Del said, "so we can update ourselves as to the current situation. That's what you're supposed to do in business, I'm told. We're supposed to have meetings at which we update. So that's what we're doing. We're updating."

Jock gave Mickey a look. "So update us, Mickey."

"You both know what the situation is," Mickey said. "We've got Bryce in custody for the murder of Mandy Dragan."

"Is he talking?" Del asked.

"He's lawyered up so he's not saying anything, but the Crown thinks they have enough evidence to take it to trial."

Jock shook his head and didn't try very hard to conceal a look of disgust. Del turned to him.

"What? You think he's innocent?"

"I think he's my nephew," Jock said. "I think we're looking for the way out of the mess we've gotten ourselves into. I'm not convinced Bryce is the way."

"What? You think one of us killed her?" This from Del, in a voice full of the impossibility of such a notion.

Jock didn't say anything. Del turned again to Mickey. "What about Dave Mackie?"

"What about him?"

"What's his status?"

"His status is we've caught him with a dead body in a shopping cart, and then he tried to run away from officers. It won't come as a surprise that he's still in custody."

"But Dave's not our killer," Del said.

"No, he didn't kill Mandy, but then there's the question of what he was doing with the body."

"What's Mackie say?" The question came from Jock.

"He says he was walking by the railroad tracks at midnight and came across the body."

"But you don't believe him?" Jock, again.

"I do not," Mickey said.

"I sent Dave out there," Del said.

Mickey didn't even try to hide his surprise. "What do you mean?"

"I mean I got a phone call saying there was something out at the Mill Pond I might be interested in. Ajey sent Dave out there. He found the body."

"You should have told me this," Mickey said.

"I'm telling you now," Del said.

"Jesus H. Christ," Mickey said.

"The point is, Dave is a bit of a ticking time bomb," Del said. "Everything starts to fall apart if he panics and shoots his mouth off."

"Like I said, we got him in custody," Mickey said. "For the moment, you're probably okay. But he has a bail hearing next week. If he doesn't get out then, that's probably when you should start to worry."

"Then let's make sure we get him out," Del said. "Who's his lawyer?"

"Some court-appointed dofus," Mickey said.

"Get him someone who knows what the hell he's doing," Del said.

"Don't look at me," Mickey said. "I arrested the son of a bitch. I can't hire a lawyer for him."

Del shook his head. "Jumping Jesus, I have to do everything myself."

"There is an argument to be made, Del, that we are in this mess thanks to certain actions you've taken," Mickey said.

"That's nuts," Del said.

"I mean why the hell would someone call you and tell you that Mandy Dragan was lying out at the Mill Pond?"

"First of all, that's not what the caller said. I didn't know she was out there."

"But you suspected. That's why you sent Dave."

"I have no idea why I got the call." Del, insistent.

"I think I do," Mickey said. "The caller was also the killer. He knew something about what you have been up to. He knew you'd get nervous and go out there and get the body and attempt to cover it up."

"But that didn't happen," Del said.

"Only because Dave screwed everything up and got caught with the body in a shopping cart."

"Great, this is just great," Jock exploded. "We are screwed here, Del, and it's your fault."

Del gave him a fierce look. "Don't hang all this on me, *Mister* Mayor. Certain questionable actions on your part play into this. Point all the fingers you want, but the fact is we will all end up in the same furnace room in hell."

"Yeah, maybe," Jock said, "but let's worry about the furnace room in hell later. For the moment, let's just try to stay out of jail."

Del worked his mouth around, as though getting it ready for what he was about to say. "You want to stay out of jail? Yeah, well, screw you, *Mister* Mayor. I didn't notice you worrying too much about jail when the money was flowing in. When you built that house out there in the country. Built it big as a g.d. hockey rink."

He thrust his face into Jock's. "So you suck it up. You don't want to go to jail? Then you g.d. make sure you don't go to jail."

Del backed away. His face softened. He let out a sigh. "Sure nobody wants a drink? Jumping Jehovah, I could use one."

Neither Jock nor Mickey said anything.

Del took a deep breath and said, "Dave said it himself. He was out for walk. He found a body. End of story as far as I'm concerned."

"Sure, Del," Mickey said. "If that's what you say happened, then that's what happened. However—"

"Don't give me a g.d. however!" Del shouted. "I don't want g.d. '*howevers*.'"

Mickey pretended he hadn't heard Del. "We've got another problem."

"What?"

"Glen Petrusiak."

"Who the hell is that?" Del demanded.

"I introduced him to you, Del. He's my partner, and he doesn't fall into line as easily as some of us local boys."

"Everybody falls into line," Del said. "Just takes a little of the right persuasion, that's all."

"I'm not so sure about Glen," Mickey said.

"Jumping Jehovah," Del said. "Everyone's on my ass today. We're all on edge. Gotta calm down. Think clearly. I really could use that drink. Am I the only one needs a drink?"

Silence in the big room. Outside, the light was lost and the Toronto skyline disappeared, as if by magic.

35

It was left to the Blessing Smile Inspector to deliver the news. Not bad news, she insisted when they met early one morning in a lovely park setting. No choking interrogation room or bland conference room this time. Children wheeling past on bicycles. The cacophonous echo of a nearby soccer game. Families out for a stroll. The beat of a world outside the narrow universe of law enforcement, a more natural background for the unnatural.

Not bad news at all, Inspector Jill Lowry repeated, accompanying the words with the kind warm, reassuring smile that most likely made her popular for these assignments. No sign of the harsh interrogator previously on view. Rather than bad news, she continued, a solution, one that accommodates everyone involved.

"I'm not certain what you mean by the word 'accommodates,'" Jean interrupted.

The blessing smile wavered ever so slightly. "It means, Jean, that we all come out of this confident a fair and honorable conclusion has been reached that satisfies all parties involved, including the Force."

"Do we want to 'satisfy all parties involved?' From my point of view, I am not anxious to ensure that Sergeant Machota is satisfied."

"Nonetheless, Jean, Inspector Duke and I have an obligation to do what's best for the Force. I'm sure you understand that."

"So what is best for the Force?" Jean felt her stomach begin to tighten, the first intimation that her worst fears were about to be realized; that this was not going to end well.

"Jean, we want to ensure that whatever you do in the future, you have the security that allows you to comfortably pursue the next phase in your life," Inspector Lowry went on. "We're offering what I believe is a very attractive package that reflects the high regard the Force has for you and your years of service."

Her stomach tightened more. She felt abruptly nauseous. "In other words, you want me out," Jean said.

"We want to do what we think is best for you at this point, Jean."

"Inspector Lowry, this man sexually assaulted me, shot me, and left me for dead on a Kandahar street."

"No one doubts you have been through a bad time, Jean, or that your life was in danger from Afghan insurgents."

"It wasn't so much the Afghan insurgents as it was Sergeant Machota," Jean interjected, trying to keep the rising anger out of her voice.

"Unfortunately, we have two very different stories about what happened that night, and no witnesses to verify either version. That leaves the Force in a difficult position. It's been decided this is the best way to resolve the issue to the satisfaction of all parties."

"And what happens to Sergeant Machota? Is he leaving the Force as well?"

"Part of the settlement involves the privacy of both parties," Inspector Lowry carefully answered.

"In other words, he remains on the Force."

The blessing smile seemed a little strained now. "I'm not really at liberty to say, Jean."

"So as a result of being attacked, saving Machota's life, and ending up shot, I am being thrown out." The words choked in her throat.

"Please don't look at it that way," Inspector Lowry said.

"What other way is there to look at it?"

"Look at it as the beginning of a new phase of your life," the inspector said. This time, the words were not accompanied by the blessing smile.

"You're a woman, can't you see what's happening here?" Jean demanded. "I'm being made a scapegoat while Machota gets off scot free. What really pisses me off, Inspector Lowry, you're complicit in all this. You're enabling them to do this to me."

Inspector Lowry regarded Jean sternly. "That's how you're looking at it, and I'm sorry you are," she said in the hard interrogator's voice from their first interview. "I look at it entirely differently. I look at it from the point of view of the Force, and for the sake of the Force this is what's on the table." She paused and took a deep breath. "Take the offer Jean, it's a good one. Take the offer, go quietly and get on with your life."

"Go to hell," Jean said.

Inspector Lowry's fine white head snapped back, as though she had been hit. She quickly recovered, though, saved by years of training in proper Force Speak. "I'm sorry that's your response, Jean. I understand that emotions are running high right now. I want you to take some time. You'll receive the details of our offer in the next day or so. Review it, and then let's talk again."

"Go straight to hell," Jean said.

Inspector Lowry stood and glared down at Jean. "Perhaps I should be telling you the same thing."

"I've already been there," Jean said. "You sent me. But now I'm back, and I'm not accepting your offer."

Something reminded her of Afghanistan. That was it. The smell of decaying leaves. Except there were no leaves in Afghanistan.

Still.

Yes, that was it. The decay. The smell of dying. Of death, Jean thought.

She opened her eyes. Her nose was pressed into dank leaves. Awful smell. She lifted herself up, groaning as pain shot through her head. She noticed crimson drops splattering against the leaves. Where did those drops come from? Then she understood these were drops of blood. Her blood. Coming from a gash in her forehead. She touched at it. Prickling pain.

She pushed herself into a sitting position. The gray day had lost much of the light it had been clinging to. In a few minutes it would be dark, and the last thing she wanted was to be out here after dark. Anything but that.

She used a nearby tree trunk to brace herself. Then, gripping the trunk, she lifted herself to her feet in a vertigo-inducing swirl of dizziness. She felt even more nauseous. She thought of all those movies in which the hero—sometimes even the heroine; Angelina Jolie kicking butt floated through her foggy head—regained consciousness in time to save the world.

Right now, the last thing Jean felt like was saving the world. She was no Angelina Jolie, not right now with her skull split open.

She forced herself away from the tree trunk. She tripped over a rock outcropping and nearly lost her balance. Gingerly she moved back down the slope, feeling disoriented, wanting to lie down and forget everything, telling herself that she couldn't do that. She had to get back to the truck. She had to get out of here.

Jean reached the path adjacent to the low stone wall by the cliff, followed it to the staircase where she paused to catch her breath, touching at her forehead, feeling the warm stickiness of her own blood. She swiped at the blood, trying to stop it from running into her eyes.

Pinpoints of light dotted the valley below, except at Jock Whitlock's place. No pinpoints there. It glowed out of the falling darkness, showcased in shimmering gold, a lightship landed from space.

When she finally reached the truck, Jean found tissues in the glove compartment, pressed a couple of them against her forehead in an attempt to stem the blood flow and avoid messing up the truck's interior. She studied herself in the rearview mirror. She must have gotten the nasty gash when she hit the ground after her assailant struck her from behind. She felt around the back of her head. A nasty egg was already growing.

She was still getting a double view of the world, feeling sick and weak. She wondered if she would be able to drive. Keeping the tissues pressed against her forehead, taking deep breaths, she spotted a water bottle in one of the console holders. She unscrewed the cap and took a drink. The water was tepid but it did the trick and revived her somewhat.

After a time, she felt strong enough to at least start the truck. Andy Williams sang "Moon River" on the radio. Bryce and his easy listening music, she thought dimly. Then she put the truck into reverse and backed out of the parking spot. That wasn't so bad, she thought. She shifted into gear as more blood trickled down her face.

She went forward out of the parking lot and started for the exit to the park.

36

With a place like this, I keep telling you, we must have help," Sharma Caulder insisted.

"Maids, butlers, all that *Downton Abbey* crap," said Del.

"You never listen to me." Sharma, at full pout. "You are so mean."

"*Downtown Abbey*, that's Sharma's favorite show. She likes that caste system, the people at the top grinding down the folks at the bottom." Del smiled at her. "Makes her feel good."

She did not smile back. "You should watch that show, and then you would see what it is like to have a little class."

"You have servants in here and they're poking into your private affairs, hearing things they shouldn't be hearing," Del continued, ignoring what Sharma had just said. "That's what that g.d. show is all about, isn't it? The g.d. servants listening at the key hole to the aristocracy."

"This is such a ridiculous conversation," Sharma said, folding her arms across her chest, and looking more miffed than ever. "You are a rich man. You should live like one. You should not live like a peasant."

Del didn't seem to be listening. He busied himself pouring a drink—the Oban Scotch he preferred, straight, no ice.

Sharma shifted her dark-eyed gaze to where Jock was sitting. "What about it, Jock? Does your wife not want you to have servants?"

"Hey, I'm the mayor of a small town," Jock said. "I can't afford servants."

"The two of you are impossible," Sharma said, throwing up her arms. "I am leaving."

"Good," Del said. "Jock and I have to talk business."

"You just want an excuse to drink," she said in an accusatory voice.

"Get me drunk enough," Del leered, "and I might even agree to servants."

"You are a horrible man!" she exclaimed before storming away.

Del stood holding the Scotch in his hand, watching his wife disappear. He shook his head. "Women," he said. "You can't live with 'em—and you can't shoot 'em."

"Do me a favor, Del. Don't repeat that in public," Jock said.

"Politically incorrect, eh?"

Jock said, "Even the rich have to watch their tongues these days."

"Watch every other g.d. thing, too," Del said, retreating to a sofa with his drink, feeling expansive.

Jock didn't let him stay in a good mood for long. "I was waiting until Sharma left," he said.

Del frowned at his drink. "What's up?"

"Not to add to our problems, but I don't want you to be surprised about this later, and then give me hell for not telling you."

"Telling me what?"

"Telling you about Jean."

"What the hell was she doing in Afghanistan in the first place? She should have been on the side of a highway in Saskatchewan handing out speeding tickets like all those other Mounties."

"Now she's here, poking into Ida's past. Which means she has been poking into *our* past."

"You haven't told her anything, have you?"

"What's there to tell?"

"That's it, exactly," Del said.

"The problem is, she's talked to Kip Cleveland. Or as he is now known, Carter Chartwell."

"What'd he tell her?"

"Thanks to Kip, she knows about Patrick Hamer."

Del noisily finished his Scotch, and put the glass down on the table beside him. "You know," he said, forcing himself to speak in a calm deliberate voice, "as if I don't have enough problems. Now I've got to start worrying about things that happened over forty years ago."

"It's probably nothing," Jock said. "Jean's got troubles of her own right now, including her mother's death and a brother in jail for murder. I just wanted to get you at a moment when we were alone and let you know. Like I said, so there are no surprises."

Del looked at his empty glass. "The world we live in, Jock. There are *always* surprises. We got these big houses, and you got that young wife, and we are the lords of our little world. But we are this far away from losing it all." He held up his hand so that his forefinger was nearly touching his thumb. "One wrong move. One g.d. wrong move and it's all over."

"So what do we do?"

Del grabbed his glass and lifted himself off the couch. "We have another drink—and we make sure we don't make any wrong moves."

He raised his glass in Jock's direction. "And the way we do that, *Mister* Mayor, we control the situation. We control your niece. Can you do that? Can you control her?"

"I don't know," Jock said.

"That's not good enough, Jock," Del said. "We've come too far to screw it all up now. So you get the job done. Because if you can't, I know people who can."

37

It was nearly ten o'clock by the time Jean arrived back at the house. They had treated her efficiently enough at Milton District Hospital Emergency, but even so by the time she saw a doctor, explained that she had fallen—ignoring the young ER guy's dubious look—waited around for a CT scan, much of the night was gone.

The x-rays showed that she had suffered a minor skull fracture, unsurprising considering the blow she had received. They insisted on wrapping her scalp wound in a head bandage that made her look like something out of *The Curse of the Mummy's Tomb*. They gave her painkillers and advised rest. She lied some more and said she would not be alone; someone would be with her.

Back at the empty house, she turned on lights, got some water, and found a chicken leg in the fridge that she promptly devoured. She drank more water and then went into the guest bedroom, shed her clothes and stepped into the shower, careful not to get her ridiculous head bandage wet. She stood there a long time, allowing the force of the hot spray to envelope her aching body, thinking.

Thinking about Uncle Jock Whitlock.

A teenage girl found alone at the foot of the escarpment near a woman's shattered body. How did that kid end up at the luxurious new home of the mayor of the town?

Good question.

Jean turned the shower off and then stepped out onto the bath mat, grabbed a towel and dried herself, feeling a little better. The painkillers they had given her worked their magic. The throbbing in her head had been reduced to a soft drumbeat. She felt loose and relaxed. The power of prescription drugs.

Before she got into her pajamas, she checked herself in the mirror, noting her puffy, purplish face, the area around her eyes darkening, a monstrous being out of a bad horror movie.

Dressed in her pajamas, she ate another piece of chicken, considered and rejected a glass of wine. Her cellphone rang. She didn't recognize the incoming number and debated whether to answer it. But then curiosity got the better of her; she swiped the phone open.

"Are you all right?" a familiar female voice asked.

"Tanya?"

"Good. I call funeral home. They give me this number."

"Are you all right?"

"I am okay. Sorry for what happened. You are nice. You should not have been hit like that."

"Where are you?"

"I cannot talk," Tanya said. "I wanted to make sure you are okay."

"I'm okay," Jean said. "But what about you? Can I come to get you?"

Tanya sounded scared when she blurted, "No! Please. Stay away."

"Are you at Jock's place? I'll come and get you."

"Please. I am so sorry. Better if you stay away."

The line went dead.

She got up and went into the bedroom, shed her pajamas and dressed in jeans and a T-shirt. Then she went back out to the truck, got in and started the engine, ignoring her exhaustion, determined and focusing. The things she did best. The things that got her into trouble. But that was fine. Tonight she was looking for trouble.

———

The escarpment loomed in the distance beyond Derry Road. Even though she had never been there before, she had little trouble finding the house. It lit the surrounding landscape.

Jean parked in the wide bricked drive fronting the four-car garage. She got out and strode to the front door, debating whether to knock, deciding no, good old Uncle Jock wouldn't mind a late night visit from his favorite niece. But when she tried the latch on the door, she found it locked. Yes, of course. When you occupied a house like this, you couldn't be too careful. You locked the doors at night, just in case the mob came for you with torches and pitchforks.

She pounded on one of the thick double entrance doors, a sharp, authoritative police officer's knock, the sort of knock that got your attention.

But not immediately. She struck the door with her fist three more times before it opened. Jock stood there, blinking uncomprehendingly. He was dressed in a soft gray tracksuit. He looked like one of the Sopranos, not a bad comparison, actually.

"Jean, what the hell?" Jock looked bleary-eyed, as if he had been drinking. "What did you do to your head?"

"Where's Tanya?" she demanded.

"What? What are you talking about? What's going on?"

"Is she here?" She pushed past Jock and found herself in a vaulted foyer overwhelmed by the staircase Clark Gable might have carried Vivien Leigh up. The newly rich apparently had seen *Gone with the Wind* and even in the twenty-first century were determined to make their houses resemble Tara.

She said, "I want to talk to Tanya, Jock."

"Hey listen, you've got to calm down." Jock had recovered somewhat from his initial shock. "I don't know who you're talking about."

"What's going on?" Jock's wife, Desiree, appeared at the top of the sweeping stairs, a 1940s movie star in a sheer robe, a long leg showing to the knee, her blond hair in disarray.

"Desiree, let me handle this," Jock snapped.

"Handle what? What the hell is this about?"

"It's nothing," Jock insisted. "Let me talk to Jean. I'll be up in a few minutes."

Desiree flounced down the stairs, artfully Jean thought, considering the high-heeled slip-ons she wore. When she reached the bottom of the stairs, she demanded, "What are you doing here, Jean?"

"I'm talking to Jock," Jean said.

"You come barging into my house at this time of night, what do you think you're doing?"

"This is between Jock and me," Jean said.

"You don't come in here like this and say that to me," Desiree flared angrily. "Who do you think you are, anyway?"

"Come on, Des, let me handle this," Jock said.

"You know, I've never liked you." Desiree was on a roll now, not to be stopped. "I know you're Jock's favorite, but you know what? I never understood it. You're a self-centered bitch as far as I'm concerned."

"Des, stop it!" Jock so loud, his voice echoed in the great hall. "I mean it. This has gone far enough. You've had too much to drink. You're saying things you don't mean."

"Me? I've had too much to drink?" Desiree was even angrier. "You should talk, you bastard. I never drank anything until I met you. God! I can't believe this."

Jock took Jean by the arm. "Come with me." He led her away.

"Where are you going?" his wife demanded. "You're just going to leave me standing here? Is that it?"

Jock pushed Jean through a door into a darkened room. He closed the door and locked it before snapping on a light.

To her amazement, knowing that Jock was not exactly the literary type, Jean saw that she was in a library, shelves filling the walls to the ceiling.

"Jock, what is this?" she asked.

"What the hell does it look like?" He looked irritated.

"Except I'm not sure you ever read a book in your life."

"It's Desiree. She thought we should have a library. She reads. All the time. She likes Nora Roberts." He stopped, seeming to remember why they came in here. "Jean, for God's sake, what are you doing to me? It's after eleven. Des is right, you shouldn't come barging in here like this. And what the hell happened to your head?"

"Someone cracked my skull up on the escarpment this afternoon," Jean said. "I was talking to your friend Tanya when it happened. When I woke up Tanya was gone. I figure you might know where she is."

"Who's Tanya? And how the hell would I know where she is?"

"She told me she was staying with you."

"You're kidding. Why would she tell you that?"

"Jock, don't lie to me."

"I'm not lying." Except he looked like he was.

"Then why would she tell me she was here?"

"How should I know? Jean, this is crazy talk. What's wrong with you lately, anyway?"

"I don't know, Jock. My brother's in jail for a murder I don't think he committed. There are two dead women, and every time I look around, there's someone associated with Del Caulder—and you."

"So what do you think? You think Del is out there murdering women?"

"I think something's going on here, Jock. What is it?"

"Something's going on? How dare you, Jean," Jock flared. "Des is right. You come in here late at night, throwing around crazy accusations. You're not a cop. You can't just come marching in here."

"I'm your niece, Jock, your nephew's in jail, and you're lying to me."

For a moment, she thought he was really going to explode. Then he seemed to catch himself. The sight of Jock fighting to stay calm was something to see. "Go home, Jean," he said quietly. "Nothing's going to be solved here tonight."

Outside, Desiree began pounding on the door. "Jock, let me in! Jock, don't do this. Let me in!"

Jean's gaze met Jock's. She looked for some sign of anything beyond the coldness in those eyes. There was nothing. "This changes everything," she said. "Nothing's going to be the same between us."

"Go home, Jean," Jock said, "The best thing right now is to just go home."

38

Half an hour before Bryce's bail hearing Monday morning, Jean met with Doc St. Jude. He reacted with surprise when he saw her bandaged head. "What happened to you?"

"My story is that I fell," Jean said.

"Is that what happened?"

"No," Jean said.

"I hope it was in pursuit of your brother's innocence," Doc said.

"I think it was, but I'm not sure."

"Well, let's see if we can at least get him out of jail this morning. I presume you are still prepared to act as his surety?"

"Yes, of course. How are our chances?"

"Like I said to you the other day, Jean, it's difficult to get bail for a client facing this kind of serious charge. But Bryce doesn't have a criminal record, he's a lifelong resident with some standing in the community—not to mention a family that's pretty well established around these parts. And of course, he's got a good lawyer working for him."

"Of course," Jean said.

"So I would say our chances are at least fair. But we will see."

"You've also been around this area for a long time, Doc."

"I'm not a native like you and Bryce. I didn't get out here until I was in my twenties."

"Obviously, I haven't been in town for a while, so I'm a little out of touch. Tell me what you hear."

A vague smile fluttered across Doc's pale features. "What I hear. Well, that could be a tall order. Depends on the subject."

"The local gossip, Doc. What am I missing?"

"The news that Del Caulder wants to rule the world."

"That's old news."

Doc's eyebrows jumped up and down. "Okay. Del wants to build a very expensive development up on the escarpment. Homes in excess of two million dollars. He will stop at nothing, apparently, to ensure that this happens."

"Stop at nothing," Jean said. "I wonder what that means."

"It means a lot of money is changing hands. A lot of people who were not rich before are going to get rich now. Del is on edge. He wants results and so far he's not getting them."

"One of those people who's getting rich wouldn't be Jock Whitlock by any chance?"

"Police officers, too, I hear." As he said this he nodded over Jean's shoulder. She turned to see Mickey Dann coming along the hall.

———————

To the surprise of Doc St. Jude, the Crown objected to Jean as surety. The assistant crown attorney handling Bryce's case, a soccer mom type in her mid-thirties named Karen Jepp, argued that Jean Whitlock had recently left the Royal Canadian Mounted Police under suspicious circumstances. "I understand through my sources that charges may yet be brought against her by the Force," Karen said.

Which came as a shock to Jean. What charges? What could they charge her with? Failing to allow a fellow officer to rape and then murder her?

Guilty as charged, she thought.

Doc recovered quickly to point out that Jean had been a member in good standing when she left the RCMP, an exemplary officer who had served the Force well in various postings over the past ten years, including assignment in Afghanistan.

"Your worship, my sources tell me that the world will come to an end in a week, but you know, I tend to be optimistic and believe that won't happen," Doc went on. "Even so, we should put the same credence in my sources as Ms. Jepp is asking the court to put in hers."

Over the objections of the Crown, Bryce Whitlock was released on one hundred thousand dollars bail. With Jean acting as surety, Bryce agreed to bail conditions that included reporting to Halton police once a week and abstaining from alcohol.

"What happened to your head?" Bryce demanded once he was released.

"Never mind that now," Jean insisted. "Just give me a hug."

Which he did, genuinely relieved to see her. "I don't want to go through that again anytime soon," he said once they were in his truck on the way home.

"Did you get any sleep in there?"

"Not much," he said. "The part of prison life they don't tell you about. It's not exactly a place that encourages a lot of sleep. I'm glad to be out—thank you, sis."

"The trick now is to keep you out," she said.

"Yes, I guess that's the trick, isn't it?" He sounded glum about the prospect.

"This will be okay." Jean made her voice sound reassuring. "You're innocent. Doc St. Jude is a good lawyer."

Bryce glanced at her as she turned onto Martin Street. "You still haven't told me what happened to you."

"Someone clubbed me over the head."

"Okay," he said slowly. "Why would someone do that?"

She was going to tell him what had happened up on the escarpment, her encounter with Jock, then decided against it. She wasn't certain what any of this meant, and telling Bryce about suspicions that might well be unfounded would only complicate things that were already complicated enough.

"The less you know right now, the better, given your circumstances," she said.

"You think keeping me in the dark is going to help?"

"For the moment, let's just be careful what we say to one another," Jean said. "I'm okay, and hopefully I'm getting somewhere proving your innocence."

"Getting somewhere. What does that mean?"

Good question, Jean thought. Was she getting anywhere at all?

39

Doris, anticipating Bryce's arrival, had once again set out Ida in the rear viewing room—Ida asleep beneath a sheet, undisturbed by her son and daughter seated nearby.

They sat in silence for a long time before Bryce began talking. He said, "They killed him for her."

Jean looked at him. "Killed who?"

"Patrick Hamer. That's the guy you've been asking about, isn't it?"

"Mom's boyfriend from Queen's University. The boy who disappeared."

"Dad was involved. So was Del Caulder, Uncle Jock, and Kip Cleveland."

"Carter Chartwell."

Bryce nodded. "Carter Chartwell. They didn't mean to kill Patrick, I don't think, but they did."

"How?"

"They took him up on the escarpment. I think they just intended to scare him, but he broke away and ran through the trees. They chased him. Patrick wouldn't have been familiar with the terrain up there. I guess he got close to the edge of the cliff, slipped, and fell over the side. They buried him up there somewhere, and then swore to each other they would never tell a soul."

"But why? Why would they do that?"

"According to what I was told, they thought Patrick raped Mom. She refused to go to the police, so they decided to take things into their own hands."

"Did Mom know this?"

"Dad told her years later, long after they married."

"She must have been devastated."

Bryce nodded again. "Here's the thing. Here's the dirty little secret she kept from everyone. Patrick never raped her."

"I don't understand."

"They had sex together, but it was consensual. But then Kip—or Carter—found out that she had been with this guy, so she lied. She said they'd had sex, but she hadn't wanted it. Kip decided that was rape, and the rest of it happened."

"What? She told Dad this?"

"After he told her what happened to Patrick."

"And how do you know all this?"

"Dad told me. Just before he died. I wish he hadn't, but I guess he felt he had to get it off his chest. He swore me to secrecy, made me promise never to tell anyone."

"But why didn't you tell me?"

"Because you were a cop, Jean. With your extreme sense of these things, I was worried about what you might do. Besides, what difference did it make at that point? Dad was dead, Mom was already descending into some form of dementia."

"Why are you telling me now?"

"Because it's distracting, and I guess I'm selfish enough that, right now, I don't want you distracted."

Jean gave him a long look before she said, "And you think, what? That I'm just going to simply forget the dirty family secret you've lied to me about all this time?"

"What choice is there? It happened so long ago. Mom and Dad, Uncle Jock, Kip, they had to find some sort of peace within themselves over what happened, and somehow they did."

"Or maybe they didn't, Bryce. At least Mom didn't."

"Now she's gone—and now you know. What does it change?"

Maybe everything, Jean thought. Maybe everything.

40

Ajey Jadu's father slipped away while Ajey sat at his bedside. The moment he was gone, Ajey's cellphone buzzed. He swiped it open. It was Del Caulder. "Del this isn't a good time," Ajey said into the phone.

"No?" Del said. "What's wrong with it?"

"I'm sitting here with my father. He just died."

Del paused a few seconds before he said, "I'm sorry to hear that, Ajey. They're releasing Dave this afternoon. Get over to the jail, pick him up and then have him bring the girl over tonight."

"Dave will go along with this?"

"Dave will do what we tell him to do. Get her here for eight."

"What about Sharma?"

"Sharma's going to be busy with the death of her father."

"I should talk to my sister," Ajey said.

"I'll talk to her," Del said. "You've got other things to worry about."

Del hung up.

Ajey put the cellphone away, fighting to tamp down his rising anger, staring at his father.

"You picked the wrong day to die, Papa," Ajey said out loud. He patted his father's cold hand. "But then maybe I'm being unfair to you. Maybe there is never a good day to die."

Sitting there, Ajey did his best to conjure emotion. All he could think was that there was now one less challenge in his life with which he had to deal. Whatever God there was knew he had enough of those on his plate these days what with Del's endlessly snarled development deals and his constant demands, including this latest and most dangerous edict.

Del was crazy. To Ajey's astonishment, his sister appeared to go along with it. Madness. But then here he was participating in the madness. Ajey, facilitator of all things. Some of them legal. A great many of them—well, better not to think about all the stuff that wasn't legal.

Ajey went out to the nurse's station to tell them he would make arrangements with a local funeral home. He went out to the parking lot, thinking that he should call Sharma—even though Sharma didn't give a damn about her father, and almost never visited him in hospital. No, he decided. He wasn't going to call. Let Del, the faithful husband, deal with that.

Once he was seated in his Jag, he phoned the Whitlock Funeral Home—nice bit of irony there! Somewhat disappointingly, neither Jean nor her brother answered. Instead, he got a pleasant-sounding woman named Doris. He explained who he was, that his father had died at Milton District Hospital. Doris said she would take care of the deceased, not to worry. Could he drop around this afternoon to firm up arrangements? Ajey said he could.

After he hung up, he drove over to the county jail and picked up Dave Mackie, who was not happy about being kept waiting. His hulking frame seemed to fill the inside of the car. He smelled of jail and unwashed men. Ajey was repulsed. He took a deep breath. He had to deal with these lowlifes. He didn't like it, but that was the job. This was life in the service of Del Caulder.

Dave was saying something Ajey didn't catch. "What's that?" he asked.

"I said my effing wife wouldn't come for me, the bitch. I could kill her."

"Hey, Dave, Del just bailed you out of jail."

"Yeah, so what? You want me to kiss his ass? Forget that he's why I ended up there in the first place?"

"The point is, you're in enough trouble." Ajey tried to keep his tone reasonable. "I don't think you should kill your wife."

"She wants me out of the house," Dave continued angrily. "I'm sitting in a jail cell and she's telling me she wants me out."

"Women," was all Ajey could think to say, although if the smell was any indication, Ajey could hardly blame Dave's wife for wanting to have nothing to do with him.

"So what is this?" Dave trained hostile eyes on Ajey. Jailhouse eyes, Ajey thought.

"What this is, Dave, is a ride home, with an opportunity thrown in."

"Yeah, right. You guys and your opportunities. Your opportunities landed me in a whole lot of trouble."

"Which we will extract you from. They've arrested someone for Mandy's murder. All you did was find the body."

"What do you want from me?"

"A little help tonight, that's all."

"What's the deal?"

"We need to make a pickup for Del," Ajey said.

"Not this again."

"We need to have her there by eight."

For a moment, Dave didn't say anything. When Ajey glanced over, he found Dave studying him closely.

"I can't figure you," Dave said. "You keep doing their dirty work for them. What the hell do you get out of it, anyway?"

"It's business, Dave, that's all. Nothing more than that. The way you have to look at it."

Dave settled back in the seat. "Sure, that's the way I look at it. Business. But he's a sick bastard."

"We're all sick bastards," Ajey said.

"To get involved in this stuff, yeah, I guess we must be," Dave said.

41

Dave and his wife, Martha, and their six-year-old daughter occupied an apartment in a small complex behind Dave's garage. A dump, Ajey decided when he dropped him off. He lived in a dump with an angry wife, and a crying kid, willing to do just about anything, because other than to fix a car Ajey supposed he didn't know anything else.

Ajey said he would pick Dave up at eight.

"That don't give me much time," Dave said.

"To do what?"

"Patch things up in there." He jerked his thumb toward the apartment.

"Just for tonight. Then you can spend the next month romancing her."

"Yeah, right," Dave said. And got out of the Jag.

As Ajey drove away, it came back to him that his father had just died, and here he was mixed up in things he shouldn't be mixed up in. He wondered if he was really any better than Dave. He just drove a better car, that's all, probably wouldn't even have that if it wasn't for his sister. He certainly dressed better, and he lived better, and he didn't have the worry of a wife ready to throw him out—not yet, anyway.

Well, he would draw the line at—what? Good question, one that he had yet to answer. Del Caulder could take over the world, at least the world west of Toronto, and Ajey wanted to be part of the conquest. In order to accomplish that, certain compromises had to be made, a few things overlooked. This was business, he kept telling himself; he was determined to do business.

When he reached the funeral home, he was surprised to see Jean Whitlock emerge from the house at the back. Of course. This is where Bryce lived. Jean would be staying here. He took note of her bandaged head. Yes, well, that was unfortunate, but unavoidable under the circumstances.

As soon as she saw him, she knew. "Not your father…"

"Yes," he said.

"I'm so sorry, Ajey."

"What can you say? He went peacefully? Yes, that was the case. I've come to make funeral arrangements. With someone named Doris?"

"That's right," Jean said. "She works with Bryce. She will take good care of you."

"And your mom, too, I heard," Ajey said.

"Not a good time for either of us," she said.

"And you've had an accident."

"It looks worse than it is," she said. She indicated the bandage wrapped around her head. "The hospital being careful."

"What happened?"

"Doing something I probably shouldn't have been doing."

Ajey forced one of his dazzling smiles. "I guess I'd better go and see Doris. I don't want to keep her waiting."

"Again, my condolences," Jean said.

"And mine to you," Ajey said.

He turned and walked toward the funeral home. Feeling Jean's eyes on him.

42

Jean thought about Ajey as she stood in the bathroom facing the mirror removing the bandage and running her fingers through matted hair. That was better. Her hair looked like hell, but that didn't make any difference, not now.

She tossed the bandages into a kitchen garbage receptacle and went to the front window. Ajey's silver Jaguar was still in the parking lot. He spent an hour inside the funeral home with Doris. By the time he left it was growing dark.

As Ajey turned his Jag onto James Street, he switched on the car's headlights. Jean, following behind in the truck, did the same. At the light, Ajey veered left into the nighttime traffic. She waited until three or four cars were between them and then followed him.

He seemed in no hurry moving south on Ontario Street. She kept him in view as he swung onto Ontario's only toll road, Highway 407, headed west. The traffic was, as usual, heavy. Again, Ajey appeared in no hurry, mostly staying out of the passing lane. Jean continued behind him, keeping her distance.

The western sky was aflame, the dying light fighting a losing battle with the coming night. It was pretty much dark by the time Ajey reached the town of Burlington and swung onto Old Waterdown Road.

This was a wooded area of Burlington, affluent homes nestled among the trees above the road. Jean saw the Jag turn right into a driveway. She slowed as she passed a pleasant one-story house. She saw Ajey get out of the car. Her quarry had arrived home.

Disappointed, Jean drove to the end of the street, turned into a drive and then backed out again, and pulled onto the shoulder so that she had a view of Ajey's house, debating what she should do. If he was home for the evening, she was wasting her time hanging around.

She was probably wasting her time, anyway.

However, a few minutes later, the front door at Ajey's house opened and Ajey appeared, backlit against the interior light. He carried a little girl in his arms. Presently, a small woman appeared by his side and took the girl from him. He bent to kiss the woman, and then came out to the Jag. Outside lights flared on as Ajey reached his car, Jean saw that he had changed from a formal business suit into jeans and a sports jacket.

She started up the truck as Ajey backed down the drive and drove away. This time he drove east on Highway 401. Traffic was still heavy, but she had no trouble keeping him in sight until he reached the Milton turnoff at Highway 25.

He took the exit and then went south on 25, finally making a right turn that took him over to Bronte Street North. Dave Mackie's garage was off to the left. She could see Dave waiting outside as Ajey's Jag came to a stop.

By the time she swung around and caught up to the Jag, it was speeding north again.

Above the 401, the traffic thinned, and Jean grew nervous that Ajey would realize someone was following him. However, the Jag didn't go far. Soon enough it turned right into a motel complex. Jean pulled over to the road shoulder and got out in time to see Dave disappear into a room at the end of the complex.

A couple of minutes later, Dave came out wrestling with a stumbling figure. Hard to tell from where Jean stood, but the figure looked small and female, no match for Dave's hulk-like strength. Ajey was out of the car, holding the rear passenger door open. Dave got the female into the back and then pushed himself in beside her. Ajey closed the door, went back around to the driver's side and got in.

Jean returned to the truck, watching through the side view mirror as the Jag rumbled onto the roadway and headed south toward Milton. Jean checked to make sure there was no oncoming traffic and then U-turned across the highway and drove after the Jag.

Ajey retraced his route but skirted the town this time, moving west on Steeles Avenue. Across Tremaine, the surrounding lights disappeared and the night closed in. The Jag rose up a steepening roadway. Momentarily, its taillights disappeared as the road twisted. But then she spotted them again, reaching the top of the hill.

A great stone house glowed against the moonless night. The Jaguar's headlights briefly illuminated an adjacent cornfield before it went through the open gate. Jean parked the truck next to the cornfield. She reached into her shoulder bag on the passenger seat and pulled out the baton. Then she got out of the truck and walked to the gate.

At the far end of the drive the Jag stopped, and the two men got out. A bulky shape that had to be Dave yanked the female out of the back.

Jean waited until the trio disappeared inside the house before going through the gate and down the driveway. A half-moon crept out from behind the clouds, lighting the coniferous trees lining the road. She moved along, staying close to the trees until she reached the house.

She passed a three-car garage, moving around the side of the house to a patio stone deck fronting an infinity pool. Jean stepped onto the deck. Sliding glass doors opened into a great room dominated by a stone fireplace.

Her eyes weren't on the magnificence of the room, however. They were on Tanya, half naked, splayed on a sofa, semi-conscious, wrapped around Del Caulder.

Jean snapped the baton out to its full twenty-six-inch length. She smashed it against the glass. She struck it again and again until the window shattered. Jean stepped through the opening and started across the living room. Vaguely, she could hear Tanya start to scream.

Dave loomed in front of her, lunging. She whacked the baton against his legs. He yelped and collapsed to the walnut floor. She whipped the baton across his head. There was an explosion of blood and teeth.

Del in a flowing beige robe struggled off the sofa, his face an interesting mixture of fear and irritation. "What the g.d. hell is going on—" and that's all that he got to say before Jean struck him. He went down, screaming.

Tanya had worked herself into a sitting position, eyes blank, her pale face showing no emotion. There was a throw on the back of the sofa. Jean grabbed it and wrapped it around the girl's shoulders.

She lifted Tanya off the sofa. "It's all right," she said. "You're safe."

"No, I'm not," Tanya said.

They started across the room, side-stepping Del writhing on the floor. Not far away, Dave lay still. Ajey came darting out of nowhere. He had a gun.

Jean poked him hard in the gut with the point of the baton. The air went out of him and he gasped, falling back, dropping the gun, trying to maintain his balance. Jean picked up the gun, stuck it in the belt of her jeans, and then cracked the baton against the base of Ajey's neck, putting him down.

Jean dragged Tanya into a foyer, saw the front door ahead, and started for it. She got the girl outside, wrapped the throw more securely around her, and together they made their way back along the roadway and through the front gate to where Jean had left the truck.

43

When Jean thought her ordeal with the Mounties was finally over, it turned out it wasn't over at all.

Jean had—what?—retreated? Escaped? Run away? Trying to find the best way to describe how she came to be in Brockville, a town along the St. Lawrence River, south of Ottawa.

She was here; that's all she knew.

A sympathetic friend with whom she had been stationed in Winnipeg had inherited an apartment above a King Street bank from her aunt. The place was furnished but unused. Jean could stay there until she got back on her feet again—or whatever it was you did when you had been through what Jean had been through.

There she was, crossing King Street, finally free after the various agonies of the last eight months, feeling she could breathe again, when the RCMP cruiser pulled up, and the two uniformed officers got out. Young, fresh-faced, typical eager-beaver Mounties, she thought, watching them arrange their faces in the friendly-but-stern manner they had been taught to adopt when confronting members of the public.

The blond officer said, "You are Jean Whitlock?"

She said, "Yes."

She didn't catch their names when they introduced themselves. Or she didn't care. What difference could it make? The blond officer said, "If you wouldn't mind coming along with us, Ms. Whitlock, it won't take long."

"What's this all about?" Jean said, giving them stern authority right back.

"Just a routine follow-up," said the dark-haired officer who appeared to be a few years older than his partner. "If you'll just step into the cruiser, we will have this over in a jiffy."

A *jiffy*? she thought. This was going to be over in a *jiffy*? She said to the officers, "How did you know where to find me?"

"Why don't you get into the car, Ms. Whitlock?" the blond officer said in a friendly voice.

Yes, all right, she thought. Let's see what all this is about.

The two officers sat in front, not saying anything. The blond officer was behind the wheel, concentrating on traffic. The officer with the darker hair appeared to be writing something on a clipboard.

They drove a short distance west along King Street, then south toward Block House Island and the St. Lawrence, wide at this point and glistening in the afternoon sunlight. She was vaguely surprised that RCMP headquarters was down here, before realizing they were not going to any headquarters.

The blond officer brought the cruiser to a stop. He stared straight ahead. But the darker-haired officer turned and said, "It's all right, Jean, you can get out here."

And then she thought, No, it couldn't be. He wouldn't do this—*they* wouldn't be part of it. But she was wrong. They *would* do this. They *would* be part of it.

She saw him as soon as she got out. He was wearing an open-necked white shirt, not tucked into the faded jeans nicely fitted to his hips. He looked as though he had lost weight as he approached. The picture of health. The sight of him set her teeth on edge.

Adam Machota said, "Thanks for coming, Jean."

She said, "Don't come any closer."

He stopped and gave her a crooked smile. "I guess I'd better be careful. Otherwise, you'll kick the crap out of me again."

"Are you out of your mind?" Jean said. "What do you think you're doing?"

"All I want to do is talk," he said. "Come on. Let's take a walk out on the island. Have you been down here? It's pretty amazing, what with the river and everything."

She looked around. The RCMP cruiser had disappeared. She swung back to him and said, "I want you to leave me alone."

"No one's going to hurt you, Jean. We're out here in public on a sunny day. A talk, that's all."

"There's nothing to talk about," she said.

"Then let's just walk," Machota said. "The river's gorgeous."

A lake freighter passed, headed east toward the Three Sisters, the islands marking the beginning of the Thousand Islands. Seagulls swooped over the wake of pleasure craft headed out of Tunnel Bay into the river. A breeze ruffled the ends of Machota's hair as he walked slightly ahead of her, the guide leading the way.

He stopped and turned to her, shading his eyes, as if to get a better view. "You look good, Jean. I heard you are doing well."

"No thanks to you," she said.

"Listen, we've both been through a rough time," he said. "I can't tell you the trouble this has caused me. But the good news is, it looks as though we've both come through the worst of it."

She stared at him, blinking in amazement. "The trouble this has caused you? Are you serious? You shot me, you son of a bitch."

"Hey, keep your voice down, Jean," Machota said calmly. "There's no need for either of us to be angry at this point. Anger isn't going to get us anywhere."

She took a deep breath and said, "You still haven't told me what you want."

"I don't *want* anything, Jean. I feel badly about what's happened. For both of us. I understand they're providing you with a medical discharge and a very generous settlement. I'm so glad to hear that. Me, they've been a lot tougher on."

"How's that, Adam? How have they made life so much tougher for you?" She felt the anger rising in her again.

"You go off to a well-earned and prosperous retirement," Machota said. "Me, on the other hand, it's back to the old slog." He gave her a sly smile. "They've assigned me to Yellowknife for my sins."

"And you're still a sergeant?"

"I'm a sergeant major."

"So they've promoted you?" Jean couldn't keep the angry astonishment out of her voice.

"I suppose they have," Machota said with a shrug. "But you know, with this Yellowknife assignment, it doesn't feel like a promotion."

"Do you have any idea at all what you've done to me?"

"I know we have both made mistakes," he said. "Things got pretty crazy over there, that's for sure. But what I want to say to you, Jean, is that we should put this behind us now so that both of us can get on with our lives."

"I don't have much choice, do I?"

"Sure you do, Jean. That's what I wanted to talk to you about," Machota continued. "We do have choices. As I say, we can put this all behind us or we can continue to make life miserable for each other. I'd like to suggest that we call a truce, you and me, and not take this any further and perhaps wreck more lives."

"What are you getting at?"

"I understand you've been talking to folks at CBC television."

"That's none of your business," Jean said.

"You see, that's where you're wrong. It's very much my business when you're making unfounded accusations against me."

"They are not unfounded."

"These are allegations that have been reviewed inside the Force and found not to have any valid basis."

"Are you kidding me? You lied through your teeth to those people."

"That's your view of the facts," he said in a formal voice. "It's not mine."

"Are you really standing here denying what happened?"

"I'm not denying we both made mistakes. I acknowledge that. But let's move forward now. Let's not go stirring up more trouble for one another."

"Goodbye, Adam," she said, the bile rising into her throat. She turned to start away.

He came after her, insinuating himself in front of her, so that she had to stop. His handsome face had gone sullen, a petulant child not getting his way.

"Don't do that," he said. "Don't you walk away from me."

"Don't touch me," she shot back at him. "Get away from me, and do it now."

He moved back a couple of paces, "Don't talk to the CBC," he said. "I mean it. If you do, it's going to be trouble, Jean. I'm warning you."

"Go to hell," she said, and pushed past him.

This time he didn't try to stop her, but he did call after her, "Do this, Jean, and you're the one going to hell—and I'm going to send you there. I swear I will. I will send you right straight to hell."

She kept walking.

44

They reached Bryce's house just ahead of the rain. The girl had said nothing on the way. She huddled in the passenger seat, her head against the window. When Jean asked again if she was all right, Tanya did not reply.

Jean brought the truck to a stop, turned off the engine, and then got out and went around to help Tanya. The girl, still uncertain on her feet, leaned against Jean as she hobbled toward the house. It had started to rain.

Inside, Jean expected to find Bryce waiting. But there was no sign of him. Jean seated Tanya at the kitchen table and then took out Ajey's gun and placed it on the counter. She went upstairs to her bedroom and retrieved one of her T-shirts. Back downstairs, she removed the throw from Tanya's shoulders and helped her into the T-shirt. The girl gave a listless smile of thanks.

"Would you like something to drink?" she asked.

"Water," she said, and Jean got her a glass. She gulped it down and Jean refilled her glass. There was a little more color in her cheeks as she put the glass on the table.

"I feel all funny," Tanya said.

"Did they give you something?"

Tanya nodded. "All sorts of things. It felt good at first, but then it got scary."

"Up on the escarpment, when I found you. Was it Ajey who came for you?"

"The Indian guy. Yeah. He hit you, and made me go with him."

"They were holding you against your will, right?"

Tanya stared off into space and for a moment Jean didn't think she was going to answer. Finally, she said, "I guess so. I don't know. I am not sure of anything."

"But they brought you over here."

"I was going to have…a better life… but that is not what happened."

"I want to call the police," Jean said. "They should handle this."

At the mention of police, Tanya's eyes widened. She violently shook her head. "No! No police. The police will do nothing. They are involved in this."

"I won't go to the local police. I will talk to the provincial police. They will handle this. You'll be safe with them."

Tanya opened her mouth to respond but then the front door opened. Bryce's voice called, "Jean? Are you here?"

"I'm in the kitchen," Jean replied.

Tanya's body tensed, her head slightly cocked, as though hearing something familiar.

"It's all right," Jean said. "It's just my brother."

Bryce came into the kitchen. Jean could hear the hard rain beating against the window over the sink. Tanya looked at Bryce and began to scream.

"That's him," she cried. "That's the man who hurt me!" She jumped up from the chair, continuing her hysterical screams.

Bryce stood rooted to the spot, as if confused by the girl's outburst. Then he spotted the gun on the counter, and quickly crossed to pick it up. He turned with the gun in his hand and cracked Tanya across the side of the head. She shrieked one more time before collapsing against the wall and sinking to the floor, unconscious.

Jean stared at Bryce, her face reflecting the shock she was feeling. "What are you doing?" was all she could manage.

Bryce had taken on a preternatural calmness as he trained the gun on her. "I don't want more craziness. We've had enough craziness."

"You're pointing a gun at me, Bryce," she said.

"Where did you get it?"

"I took it away from Ajey Jadu."

"At Del's place."

"Yes."

"That's where you found Tanya?"

Jean nodded.

"Listen to me, Jean. Listen carefully, okay? Before you act or do anything rash, I want you to listen. This is going to be fine. We just have to keep our heads, that's all."

"Is that all we have to do, Bryce?"

"This girl can put me in jail for the rest of my life," Bryce said. "I made mistakes, I'm the first to admit that, but there's nothing I can do now to change that."

"What have you done, Bryce?"

"Shawna and I got involved with this girl here, this Tanya, do-ing some things we shouldn't have done. She was supposed to be for Del—and his wife, too. A play toy for them. Shawna was sup-posed to take care of her."

"So in addition to Del, you and Shawna used her, too," Jean said.

"It was Shawna's idea, not mine. Tanya didn't mind. That's what Shawna said. I went along. I shouldn't have but I did. Mis-takes. Things I regret. But now we need to make this right, Jean, and you can help me do that. You're my sister, I love you. You have to help me."

Jean took another deep breath. "What do you want me to do?"

"It's very simple. We take her up on the escarpment. That's where she has been hiding out, right? You brought her home from Del's, but then she ran away again. That's what she's been doing since she got here. Hiding up on the escarpment. So she goes back there. It's dark. She's careless. It's an accident. She slips and falls over the cliff."

"You know what you're asking me to do?"

"I'm asking you to do what's necessary, to help me. That's what I'm asking you to do. Begging you."

He kept the gun trained on her. She saw the look in his eyes. Had she seen that look before? Mad, desperate—a man who would do anything to save himself. No, she did not think she had seen anything like that before.

Until now.

"The Lincoln is outside," Bryce said. "Get her out to the car."

"I can't do it," Jean said.

"Yes, you can, Jean. You're strong. You're stronger than all of us when it comes down to it."

"You don't think there's another way?"

"What am I supposed to do, Jean? Turn myself in? You know what that means. Is that what you want?"

Jean couldn't think; everything was a blur of indecision. Tanya groaned. Her head was bleeding. Jean got a clean kitchen towel and held it against the wound. Bryce moved impatiently behind her. She noticed he always kept the gun in view—trust with a gun.

Jean lifted Tanya off the floor and then half-carried, half-dragged her out to where Bryce had parked the Lincoln. It was raining steadily. Bryce was right behind her with the key that popped open the trunk. She looked back at him. "We're not going to put her in there."

"That's the best, the safest," he insisted.

As gently as she could, Jean lowered the girl into the trunk's cavity. Tanya groaned again, her head moving back and forth. Bryce was right behind her, magically producing a roll of duct tape. "Use this," he said.

"Bryce, no. Come on."

"Use it," he demanded. That strange look in his eyes again. "Her hands and her mouth. Hurry."

She went to work, using her teeth to bite off sections of tape. She covered Tanya's mouth and then moved her hands together and wrapped the tape around her wrists. When she was finished, she stood back, breathing hard. Bryce stepped forward and slammed the trunk lid down.

"Let's go," he said.

45

"We had a fight," Bryce said as Jean drove the Lincoln through the rainy night, his voice rising above the soft electronic slap of the windshield wipers. Through the windshield, headlights illuminated the road winding toward Rattlesnake Point. Bryce held the gun nestled in his lap. He kept saying he trusted her, that she was his sister and he loved her, but he held the gun at the ready. Just in case he decided he couldn't trust her.

"We were at Shawna's apartment when it happened—the fight, I mean," Bryce explained.

She seemed to be floating through the night, silence except for the windshield wipers and the rush of air outside—and the sound of her brother's voice.

"Shawna had brought Tanya along, a playmate from the Ukraine, imported by Del for fun and games. We'd been drinking. Tanya had some pills. It was late. I'm not sure where the rage came from. I hit her. Too hard. She hit her head, and she was gone. I couldn't believe it. Neither could Tanya. I convinced her that we had to get rid of Shawna, otherwise they would send her back to the Ukraine and prison. She was traumatized, I could tell that. But she helped me. We got the body into the car and we drove up to Rattlesnake Point, and I pushed Shawna over the edge, so that it would look like an accident.

"That's when Tanya disappeared. I searched for her, but she was gone into the darkness. I knew you were at the house, that I couldn't stay too long, so I left. No matter what had happened to her, I was pretty certain Tanya wouldn't say anything, and, of course, when she showed up at the bottom of the cliff, she didn't."

"She was in shock," Jean said. "She still is."

"Maybe so, but it's too dangerous. We shouldn't take the chance. This is better. Then we don't have to worry."

We, Jean thought as she drove. Now it was *we* shouldn't take the chance. Now he had drawn her into this, much the same way he had drawn Tanya. This was her brother—her *brother* for God's sake. How could this be?

She swallowed the bile rising in her throat and said, "What about Mandy Dragan?"

"What about her?"

"Why was it necessary to kill her?"

"This is going to sound more callous than it should," Bryce said. "But if I'm being honest, I would say it was easier to kill her then to put up with her alive. Alive, it was a matter of time until she started saying things that would only get me in trouble. So that night in the basement of the funeral home—well, it is a place of death, isn't it?"

He stopped and for a time Jean thought he was finished. Then he said, "I thought it was quite inspired, actually—anonymously phone Del and tell him where I had dumped Mandy's body. I figured he would never go to the police, that he would make her body quietly disappear and that would be the end of that."

"Except it didn't quite work out the way you expected," Jean said.

"No, it didn't," Bryce agreed. "But now everything is going to be all right."

The headlights of the Lincoln swept the entrance to the park. They went through, along the roadway into the parking lot. He directed her to stop near the pathway that would take them to the cliff edge. "We're almost there," he said in a reassuring voice. "This is nearly behind us."

She got out of the car thinking, this was never going to be behind them. This would haunt them for the rest of their lives.

Gusts of wind drove sheets of rain across the parking lot as Jean opened the trunk. Bryce held the gun in one hand, a flashlight in the other. Uncertain light illuminated Tanya squirming in the trunk.

"She's awake," Jean said.

Bryce said, "Get her out. Let's not waste time."

Jean lifted Tanya up. The girl was only semi-conscious. Blood streamed down the side of her face, soaking her T-shirt. Jean got her out of the car. Tanya sank against her. "Oh, God," Jean gasped.

"Come on," Bryce ordered. "Bring her along."

Jean held the girl tightly, propelling her forward. The light from Bryce's flashlight wavered, finally discovered the pathway they would follow. As they moved toward the cliff, Tanya began to realize what was happening and made louder whimpering sounds, fighting weakly against Jean.

The light from the flashlight outlined the low stone wall and the iron railings that marked the staircases descending the cliff. Tanya made terrible noises despite the tape covering her mouth. The rain washed blood from her wound down her face. She violently shook her head and tried to pull away from Jean.

Bryce came to a stop near the edge of the cliff, or what Jean suspected was the edge. In the dark and the pouring rain, it was hard to tell. With a sudden, unexpected show of strength, Tanya twisted away. She staggered a couple of feet and fell to her knees. Bryce swore and lunged at her. Jean yelled, "Bryce! No!"

She jumped between her brother and Tanya. "We can't do this," she said.

Bryce's hair was plastered against his face twisted with anger that made him nearly unrecognizable. "What do you suggest we do? We're here, Jean. It's happening. It's too late."

"No." Jean pushed right back. "We're not going to do this."

Bryce smashed her with his gun. Jean gasped in pain staggering away, losing her balance and falling into the soft wet leaves carpeting the ground.

Momentarily she was in darkness. She could hear Bryce's heavy breathing somewhere above her, Tanya sobbing. Everything was blurry and ill formed. Her hands clawed at the leaves, fingers finding the rock. Her fingers wrapped around its cold, hard wetness. She rose through the rain and there was Bryce. She raised her arm up and her hand was filled with that rock.

She hit him with the rock and then hit him again and again and again.

And again.

Disbelief filling his face, he staggered back, regained his footing and started to raise the gun. Then a figure swiped past Jean. She had a watery glimpse of Tanya leaping onto Bryce, smashing against him, the two of them disappearing into the darkness.

Gone.

Jean dropped the rock. The rain poured down. Lightning cracked over the valley accompanied by a roar of thunder.

46

At dawn, the rain was reduced to a light drizzle. Jean sat wrapped in a blanket in the command post trailer the police had moved into Rattlesnake Point.

Jean had stripped out of her wet clothes and they found a dry pullover with HALTON POLICE emblazoned on it, and a pair of track pants that were too big for her. She leaned back so that her head rested against the trailer wall, sipping at the terrible coffee someone had brought her, trying not to think.

Mickey Dann stepped in, head drenched, wearing a long rain slicker that made him look like a character in a Sergio Leone western. Jean didn't say anything, but watched as he removed his rain gear and shook it out. He put the coat to one side and came over to where she was sitting.

"Can I get you anything?"

She showed him the coffee cup.

"Look, no one wants this to be more difficult than it already is."

Jean refused to look at him. She focused on a spot at the back of the trailer. "What's that mean?"

"It means we're buying your story."

"You're *buying* my story?"

"That Bryce dragged you and Tanya up here. You tried to save Tanya. She attacked him. She and Bryce fell over the cliff."

"That's not my story. That's what happened."

"Fair enough. That's what happened."

She forced herself to look at him. "How much did you know about Tanya?"

"I had no idea she was involved with Del, if that's what you're getting at."

"Come on, the number of times you must have been at Del's place, and you didn't see anything?"

Mickey took a breath and said, "After we found her up here, we tried talking to her but it was no dice. So we turned her over to Child Welfare. That was the last I heard of her until this morning."

"So what are you going to do with Del?"

"Detective Petrusiak has gone to his house and is bringing him in for questioning. But I wouldn't hold my breath that much of anything is going to happen. I'm sure Del's going to be lawyered up big time for this."

"Besides, he has the police on his side, doesn't he?"

"I'm not on anybody's side," Mickey said, showing his irritation. "Particularly when it comes to the abuse of underage females. But we are going to need more evidence than we've got right now. Unfortunately, the evidence went over the side of the cliff."

"So everyone gets away with everything," Jean said in a resigned voice.

"No, thanks to you, we have solved the murders of two women. Bryce didn't get away with anything."

"But a young girl who deserved better is also dead," Jean said.

"Yes," said Mickey. "That is the tragedy."

Epilogue

You look like you've lost weight," Jock said. "Have you been eating properly?"

As if to make up for any food shortage, he passed Jean a tuna sandwich. It was an uncharacteristically warm autumn day. The leaves were gone from the trees around the park in front of the old town hall. Jock was wearing a poppy in the lapel of his blue suit. In a few days' time Jock would oversee Remembrance Day ceremonies at the cenotaph. His annual recital of *In Flanders Fields* was always a highlight.

"What's a bespoke suit?" Jean asked.

"What?"

"A bespoke suit. When you sat down you pointed out you are wearing a bespoke suit. What is it?"

"A made-to-measure suit," he explained. "But a *true* made-to-measure suit, cutting an original pattern that is strictly for you. Multiple fittings to ensure the suit fits *you* properly. It's a process."

"I can imagine," Jean said.

"I only wear it on special occasions."

"Like when you're having lunch with me," Jean said.

"No question."

"Trying to make amends."

"Am I trying to make amends?"

"Are you?"

"Maybe I'm trying to have a sandwich with my niece, like old times."

"It can't be like old times."

"No?"

"For one thing, I don't like tuna sandwiches."

"Sorry, I forgot." He busied himself unwrapping his sandwich. "Listen, I never touched that girl Tanya. I tried to help her. So did

Des. We thought she was a housekeeper. Nothing more. After they found her on the escarpment, we had her at our place out of concern for her safety."

"Because of Del?"

"She was a kid, lost in a strange land. We wanted to help, that's all. But it didn't matter. She was scared. She ran away, which is when you found her."

"You knew what Del was doing."

"I *suspected*. I didn't know. Not for sure. I mean I heard things, rumors. But I had a hard time believing any of it. Nonetheless, I tried to talk to him."

"Did you?"

"Yes, I did, Jean. I warned him that if what I was hearing was true, it meant big trouble. He could forget any ideas about an escarpment development. Del, of course, being Del, didn't listen. So here we are where we are."

"Del getting away with murder."

"Come on, Del didn't murder anyone." Jock licked tuna salad off his fingers. "He tried to cover up stuff, and he's paying the price for that. Whatever happens, Del is ruined. Kaput. The escarpment development isn't going ahead. The RCMP is investigating him. I hear Sharma's thinking about leaving him. I don't think that will happen, mind you. Sharma's had to look the other way many times over the years. This is going to be one more look the other way."

"What about you, Jock? Are you worried?"

"Worried? Why should I be worried?"

"Are you going to testify against Del?"

"I hear Del wants you charged with assault and criminal trespass," Jock said.

"After I found him with a naked, drugged teenager," Jean said.

"I'm not saying anything's going to come of it. I'm just telling you what I'm hearing."

"Thanks a lot," Jean said.

"It might not be a bad idea to get of town for a while," Jock said.

The other shoe had dropped. "So that's why you insisted on lunch."

"Listen, Bryce is gone, sadly, and I hear you're selling the funeral home."

"I have sold the funeral home," she amended.

"So there's nothing to keep you around here. You've got no ties to this place. You never liked it to begin with."

"I'm not going anywhere," Jean said. "I'm staying right here."

"Why?"

She didn't want to tell him that she was staying because she could not for the moment think of anywhere else to go. What did that say about her? A woman who left the RCMP under a cloud who couldn't even muster the energy to leave town.

Aloud she said, "I've got some unfinished business here."

"What kind of business?" Jock demanded.

Jean concentrated on her sandwich. She didn't say anything.

"Jean, what kind of unfinished business?"

Still nothing. Jean stared at the sandwich for a while longer before putting it to one side. "Funny," she said. "I don't think I'm hungry today."

She got up from the park bench and started away.

"Jean?" he called.

She paused and then came back to stand over him, blocking the sunlight, throwing him into shadow. He squinted up at her. "What is it, Jean?"

"Did you kill Patrick Hamer?"

"Patrick Hamer?" Jock appeared genuinely taken aback. "You're kidding me."

"I want to know if you and my father and Carter Chartwell killed him."

Jock didn't say anything for a time. "Are you asking me as a police officer or are you asking me as your mother's daughter?"

"I'm no longer a police officer."

"Yeah? It seems to me you've spent a lot of time lately acting like a cop."

"Quit jumping around the question, Jock. I need to know."

"God, Jean. You don't need to know. Knowing isn't going to change one damn thing."

"Jock."

"Nobody killed anybody. What happened wasn't supposed to happen. What happened was an accident. We only wanted to scare the guy."

"But it was more than that," Jean said.

"It was a very long time ago," Jock said. "If it's any consolation, your mother never knew."

"That's where you're wrong, Jock. I believe she did. My father eventually told her, and it haunted her all her life, so much so that even as she faded away, even as her mind deserted her, she could never shake the guilt over her part in Patrick's death."

Jock was silent for a time. "If she knew, I certainly wasn't aware of it," he said finally. "And I'm always suspicious when it comes to stuff about being haunted by the past. The past is the past. It fades. You get on with things."

"Not in Mom's case," Jean said.

"You wanted to know, Jean, now you know."

She looked at him for a moment longer, and then turned and walked away. His voice trailed her, "Jean, don't be like this. Jean…"

She passed a municipal garbage container. She tossed the tuna sandwich into it, just as a car pulled up to the curb in front of her. A figure got out of the passenger side.

Adam Machota smiled, and started toward her.

Acknowledgments

Each November I drive to Florida with Kim Hunter. In addition to being a long-time funeral director and the neighbor who lives across the street from my wife Kathy and me in Milton, Ontario, Kim has become one of our dearest friends.

On the road south for the last couple of years, Kim has conducted an ongoing course in the techniques and rituals of the funeral business he knows so well. I couldn't have done this book without his help and guidance. The same is true of Kim's wife, Rebecca, also a funeral director, who runs the J. Scott Early Funeral Home in Milton.

If anything Rebecca is even more passionate than her husband about ensuring the living move as comfortably as possible through the sad journey that is saying goodbye to a loved one. Rebecca read the manuscript, made comments, and corrected mistakes.

However, any mistakes or shortcomings in *The Escarpment* are not the fault of Rebecca and Kim. They land squarely at the feet of the author.

As always, I must thank my wife Kathy, first reader, and the person who daily reminds me that the best thing we can all do in the face of death is live life to the fullest.

Longtime friends and editors, David Kendall in Canada and Ray Bennett in London, England, once again happily made my life miserable, thereby forcing me to write a much more readable novel than I would have otherwise.

Alexandra Lenhoff, an editor with whom I have done many books over the years, returned to the team for this novel and did what she's always done—helped me make it better.

Ric Base, without whom none of this would be possible, handled the technical aspects of producing *The Escarpment*, while bril-

liant graphics designer—and Milton Film Festival founder—Jennifer Smith worked her magic on the cover.

Thanks also to Miriam and Peter Haight at the Dorland-Haight
Gallery who generously allow a poor starving author to stand in
front of their store with a book in his hand and a hopeful smile
on his face.

Finally, many, many thanks to the friends and neighbors who
have made living in Milton such a pleasure. I hope they forgive me.

Coming Soon

THE MILL POND

Jean Whitlock must deal with a former colleague out to destroy her life while once again being drawn into murder and a small town's secrets in Ron Base's continuing series of Milton Mysteries.

And Don't Miss

THE SANIBEL SUNSET DETECTIVE MYSTERIES

Tree Callister is a private detective on Sanibel Island, off the west coast of Florida. Everyone thinks Tree is crazy to be a detective on an island where nothing ever happens. But plenty happens to Tree. In fact, he can't seem to keep himself out of trouble. Fast-paced, suspenseful, with lots of humor, mystery, and local color, Ron Base's Sanibel Sunset Detective mysteries are Florida bestsellers. All six novels are available either in print or as e-books on Amazon.

Available now as an Amazon e-book

THE SANIBEL SUNSET DETECTIVE GOES TO LONDON

Coming in November

HEART OF THE SANIBEL SUNSET DETECTIVE

www.ronbase.com
Read Ron's blog at
www.ronbase.wordpress.com
Contact Ron at
ronbase@ronbase.com